Albert, Himself

Albert, Himself

A NOVEL BY

Jeff W. Bens

DELPHINIUM BOOKS

harrison, new york   encino, california

Published in the United States by
DELPHINIUM BOOKS, INC.,
P. O. Box 703, Harrison, New York 10528

Library of Congress Cataloging-in-Publication Data
available upon request

ISBN 1-883285-22-4

First Edition

10 9 8 7 6 5 4 3 2 1

Distributed by HarperCollins Publishers
Printed in the United States of America on acid-free paper

Book design by Krystyna Skalski

For my parents

Albert, Himself

1

Albert weaving, two weeks before his daughter's third birthday, three weeks before the Delancy wedding, on a wobbly barstool in the Quarter. Beside an old man, who's talking at him, Albert Fitzmorris half-listening, holding a third John Jameson at his chin.

The old man's in a hat like Albert's da used to wear, only it not stinking of fish.

"... then and only then, I like to add in some white pepper. Then and only then, after it has set a while, I lay in the cayenne."

The old man gulps at the whiskey, Albert gulps as well. Steadies himself with a hand to the bar edge, the old man seeming to drift away.

"You could add in a little ginger root," Albert says, trying to be polite—he'd been interested at first, at the mention of gumbo—to uphold his end of the conversation, to forget, through involvement, why he's come.

"Then I—ginger root!" The old man wipes at his mouth with a sleeve. "What kind of new-wave new-age half-assed half-baked idea is that? Ginger root!"

The whiskey burns his stomach. Closing his eyes. Audrey there, a newborn baby. So small, and now she will be three. He'd make things right. Soon. Crimps his eyes tighter.

His daughter floats away, out into the blackness and the ripples of red. "I only meant—"

"Why not throw in a little chicory or a little horseradish while you're at it? Or maybe some sneezing powder or something?"

"I only—"

The old man slams the bar, whiskey jumping from Albert's glass. "Cayenne pepper!"

"I—"

"PEPPER, PEPPER, PEPPER—" The old man buries his whiskey. "And only the PEPPER!" His voice softens, "Buy us a drink, will you, son?"

Albert nodding, at the bartender, at the old man, his arm feeling rubbery, the trumpeter in the corner of the French Quarter barroom emptying spit from his horn. He's had a double Jameson for each of her years, and somehow he thinks this is what his father might have done but it is not working for him. With the next whiskey, he'll have had as many drinks in the hour as he's had in the month.

"I'm only suggesting you might *add* in a little—" his whole body feeling rubbery, like a dead fish picked up by the tail.

"—A little ginger root?"

"Yes. A little . . . ginger—" discovering the whiskey in

2

his hand, the whiskey hovering just above the bar. Raising it, tipping his head, "—root."

Tipping too far, tumbling off the barstool, his feet pedaling back until he is ten feet from it. The edge of the bar seeming liquid.

Leaning against a post.

The old man leaping to his feet. "You're drunk, sir!"

And the barroom's slowly spinning.

Trying to stop it from doing so. Pressing his cheek to the post, focusing on the fans that whirl above his head. He spins his eyes clockwise with the fans. Bad. He spins his eyes counterclockwise against the fans. Worse.

Spinning. The Delancy wedding: he does not know Jimmy Delancy's granddaughter well, she being just twenty, but his ma and Father King and Jimmy Delancy—and he wished her well of course, Jimmy's Kara—and Audrey and why she would not be there.

The back of his head rolls along the post that props up the ceiling of the bar that had once stored munitions for Andrew Jackson. A screw in the post, and his eyes peel open. Rubbing the back of his head, his weight shifting, he turns his eyes to the barroom window.

Out the window, the French Quarter alley spreads before him, the New Orleans night, the damp stone streets, the spire of the St. Louis Cathedral, with its three small crosses, the blue-lit steps of the Blue Royale Hotel. Head rolling, bar receding, lights off the glasses, red, and the bottles blurring pink.

Lids pulling down. Head bobbing. Then up. Focusing. Focus: bar edge is solid; the fan's got a mini Ireland 32 flag stuck in it; a convertible Jaguar's pulling up to the steps of the Blue Royale Hotel. It was Terry's idea, to drink it out, his blues, Terry saying this morning at work that a drunken man will always find the sober truth. But the only truth Albert had found was the one he'd carried in, that soon his daughter would be three.

Streets blur, then fast, fast into focus again. His breath nearly taken. Out from the Jaguar steps a short business-man, no more than Albert's five feet seven inches, the lights catching off his neat, grey suit, and he's opening the passenger door for an angel, who's back-lit in sapphire, the rain in silver at her feet.

He's never seen anything like her. Running a hand through his hair, down across his damp face. Moving toward the window. Staring.

The man's got his hands at the woman's thin waist, on her shoulders, through her gold hair. She wears a white dress. The man tries to kiss her neck. Her shoulders are bare.

Hands pressed against the panes of the barroom win-dow, face so close to the glass that his breathing fogs it, he thinks she may be an angel or a dream brought on by the drink and then, when he is sure that she is not, when he is sure that the light and the grace are real, he feels sud-denly sober, realizes why he has come to this bar, a bar that he thought he'd chosen because Terry had said it was quiet and Irish and cheap.

She turns her face. She's heading up the hotel's steps, her long legs floating. The Jag man follows close, stuffing money into the hand of the guy who spins the door.

Staring after them.

The spin of the doors. The couple disappearing into the blur of the hotel's lobby. And then the street's going blurry, and the window itself, and Albert's eyes looking back at him and they are not like Audrey's, hers are brown like Eileen's and his own ma's, but Audrey's hair is his and Audrey's nose, and he sees his daughter's smile, a newborn in her crib behind the viewing glass, and someone laughs from the bar behind him and when his forehead cracks the windowpane, across from the now empty hotel steps, he can somehow still see the woman, bathed in blue, the crosses of the Cathedral behind her. Turning, he feels his skin cut, and the bar dips way down and Albert sees the red behind his eyes and then only black.

Siren lights spinning in the French Quarter alleyway, from an ambulance up on the sidewalk, its back door open wide. The bartender and the old man holding open the barroom door, Albert strapped in a stretcher, moaning, wheeled out by two unhappy firemen.

There's a cut on his head where it hit the floor and his

nose is packed with cotton. But he is just drunk and it's his knee that hurts and he will not go through those ambulance doors.

All for whiskey.

A small crowd has gathered. Two people take photos from a carriage behind a mule in a flowered hat. Trying to hide his face with his hands. The ambulance's opened back blinking. Shutting his eyes against the siren's swirl.

"I won't go in there." Fighting at the straps. "Sandy!"

He should not have mentioned to the old man that he'd had alligator chili, that he'd had it at of all places a fire station, that Engine Nine made it that way on the first of every month. Then they might have just thrown him in the alley. Then he might have just walked home alone.

The lights inside the ambulance make his stomach feel alternately too big and too small. The cover of a New Orleans Saints' thermos bottle unscrewed above him, the hands calmly pouring a capful.

"Sandy—"

The coffee wets the underside of the hovering mustache, the lips sipping, not a word spoken, and then Albert regains himself, in the silence behind the sealed door, in the familiarity of his brother's droopy face.

He tries to sit up.

"Get me out of this goddamned thing, Sandy." He almost smiles.

Sandy dabs at his mustache, clucks from his lips, sips a little more, then releases the stretcher straps.

"My own brother laid out on a barroom floor." Sandy chuckles. "Jesus, Albert, who'd you hit?"

He tries to sit up again, collapses backward.

"I think my leg's broken."

Sandy shakes his head. "Point your toes."

Albert's toes stick out from beneath the blanket.

"Now wiggle them—"

"Oh, come on, Sandy."

Sandy still shaking his head. "Well, if it's not broken, it will be when she's got through with you."

Albert's vision briefly clearing. "Oh, Jesus, Sandy, don't tell *her.*"

"You won't be able to keep it from her, Al . . . " Sandy hands him a capful of coffee, drops into a voice reserved to speak about mystics and saints. "Ma knows everything."

Both brothers briefly shut their eyes.

But his ma'll think he's been with Eileen. It's for the best that she does, with his father now gone and the Delancy wedding closing in. And maybe soon he will have something to tell Sandy and his ma, about a vision in the light of the spire, a miracle maybe—and their happiness when they meet her—and he's feeling better, despite the nosebleed and the drink.

He opens his eyes.

"Hey Sandy?"

When he gets home he'll take off his shoes so as not to wake her.

"Yeah?"

"Hit the siren will ya?"

And Sandy's laughing. The siren wails, and the lights from inside the ambulance meet in the windows those from the street, the lights dancing, the tops of telephone poles now soaring by, dark crosses and light, and he shuts his eyes and sees red and cool blue and they are the tops of riverwaves, balancing shipmasts and booms, and then Albert is laughing too, in the siren's wail; pressing back the darkness that is above him and below.

SUN NOT UP. Albert sits across from his ma, in his father's old place at the long, wood table, in front of a cup of coffee, his chin cradled in his hands. No eyes meet. No words spoken. Only the sip at his coffee, and his ma slurping cereal from a spoon.

Sip—slurp, slurp, slurp—sip.

Yawn.

He seizes the opportunity. "Why don't you go back to bed, Ma? It's not even six."

"I'm not tired." A hint of County Clare in her voice, the hint that comes when she's something soon to say. Lately, she seems to have him on her mind.

"Can I make you some eggs?"

She shakes her head, straightens her plaid robe. The light from the Singer burning behind her. When he woke she was already working.

Albert frowns. He gets up, pours the remaining coffee into his thermos from the drip pot on the stove.

Runs a hand through his hair. "Ma, I—"

"You're thirty-five years old, Albert. You're a fine son. You don't have to explain yourself."

Frowning more so, head in the fridge, layering food up along his arm. His knee aches; he's a cut on his forehead that he'd tried to cover with hair.

"But I haven't seen Audrey or Eileen in the house since I can't remember when." She's up from the table. "And I'm starting to wonder if I ever will."

Moving faster than is even usual, Dori Fitzmorris, crossing to the old Singer that's pressed against the front room's far wall. The house is four rooms, the long skinny kitchen separated from the long skinny front room by the line between the linoleum and the worn wood floor, two bedrooms packed in the back. A shotgun house, not far from the river, the whole thing up on blocks.

She sits. "You've got a cut on your forehead. Coming in at I don't know what hour. If at your age, Albert, you're going to take to catting around, well, I don't know if I can stand it."

He shuts his eyes. "'Course not."

He's sawing slices from a loaf, a good loaf, he picked it up himself at the Roundelle Bakery. Opens his eyes again before he takes off his thumb. Spreads the bread with brown mustard, layering on the provolone cheese, the rough cuts of andouille sausage. Cherry tomatoes, slicing them paper thin, despite his shaking hands, the way he likes them, so that they cover the meat without hanging out the edge. He wraps the sandwich into a brown-paper bag.

Through the kitchen window the sun rises up over the long row of houses, across the shoulders of the neighborhood stray who's beginning her rounds for scraps.

He leans unsteadily over his ma, kisses her cheek. "Don't worry about me, okay, Ma?

"You got mustard on your sleeve."

Above the Singer, a picture of John Paul II and a 1972 photo of Sandy and Albert on a trawler with their da who has his enormous arms across the shoulders of his sons. They'd always called him da, at his insistence—his Irish-born father was da, and his father's father. The cousins who sent Christmas cards from Wicklow did not call their fathers da, nevermind the kids of New Orleans. But his had, and so it was.

The robe beneath the mechanism, her hands flat on the shiny cloth. "You seeing her tomorrow then?"

He straightens up. "Eileen?" He turns from her. "'Course, Ma." For a while she hadn't mentioned Eileen much, accepted how Eileen was busy with her new job. But lately

Eileen, too, seemed a part of what was on his mother's mind. "It's Saturday, isn't it?"

He lifts his blue windbreaker from its peg beside the door-frame cross. He does not meet her eyes.

"And Audrey?"

Fooling with the jacket's zipper, his fingers feeling thick. The emerald in the crux of the cross.

She does not need his troubles. The shame of his failing that could wake him in the night. What his father would have said.

Eileen lived now on the edge of the Quarter, in a neighborhood that had never been good, in a building with a metal-grated door across its entrance, with the sunlight not even reaching where Audrey slept. Sometimes he'd bring Audrey by the house to see his ma. But with Hank, this had become more difficult.

Hank had moved in with Eileen, at Easter, as if they were married.

He cannot look at her. "See ya, Ma."

Eileen was not married to Hank. Soon enough, Hank might be gone.

Three steps to the door.

And he'll tell his ma, soon, about the woman that he saw on the blue steps beneath the three crosses. Soon enough, he'll have something good to say.

"Have I shown you the dress I'm making for little Audrey?"

And he's picturing that woman beside him and they're walking along the river with her arm through his, throwing bread to the gulls like he and Eileen had done one time, only now it would be different.

"Albert?"

Smiling. "About two dozen times."

"All right for you."

She lifts the half-finished dress from the sewing basket at her feet.

He puts his hand around her shoulder, thin beneath his palm. Since his father's death, she'd become thin. "It's beautiful, Ma."

"I need to get it finished up, what with her birthday just two weeks away." She tugs at the dress's left sleeve. "Maybe we'll have them over, Al. Eileen and you, and maybe Sandy and Colleen. For Audrey's birthday. Three years old already—" Her voice goes quiet.

The sun on the street, the ride on the streetcar, the fish that need cleaning for the weekend restaurant rush.

"We'll see, Ma."

Moving again for the door.

"Eileen's awful busy."

Reaching for the handle.

"It's not for two weeks." She pulls the stitch from the dress. "Give her a little notice." When the door opens he sees her face clearly with the daylight, the unfamiliar sadness in her eyes.

Nodding. And stepping out. Into the humid New Orleans dawn, leaving the sausage ends for the stray, who's two houses down, licking out a can.

Sun rising, up over St. Charles Avenue. Albert on a downtown streetcar, the sun catching the brass and polished wood of the restored deco train. Sitting alone, at 5 A.M., heading into the Quarter.

The streetcar. The conductor. Albert. A man asleep. A drunk who talks to no one in the corner.

The drunk yells. Albert glances over. The drunk nods off. As Albert turns back, his eyes catch one of the advertisements that line the streetcar's arched, tin ceiling: pink stone steps and an elegant couple heading up them, to the opened door of an exclusive French Quarter hotel, the hotel lit up so that its windows glow gold—"The Pinnacle House. Step into Luxury."

The streetcar stops. The businessman coughs, the conductor spits, the drunk gets off. The fare box clicks, the power lines hum, the stop is empty and the streetcar moves on.

Motionless, the sun on the back of his neck, staring into the ad; and seeing her beside him, bathed not in blue now but in that gold, on the pink stone steps, curled in his arm.

• • •

BOBBY KELLY'S fish market, a wood sign: Bobby's boyish face on the left side, announcing in letters across the right, "Shrimp, crawdad, grouper, red, monk, cat—You want fresher, catch it youself." The *r* never there, business steady for thirty years, Bobby not risking a change.

Fish beds spill out onto the French Quarter sidewalk, Albert inside, in black rubber waders, loading gutted fish onto big beds of ice, his bare hands deep inside their gills.

"But she was like a vision, I tell you, Terry. A vision. I was standing there and she appeared."

Terry, in gloves, the rubber as thick as the waders, wiping his brow on his arm. 6 A.M. and they're already sweating. Behind, in the back of the market, the early customers, the buyers for restaurants, tagging fish to be loaded and delivered.

"Jesus, Albert, you're not a drinker," Terry says. "You can't trust it."

Mrs. Bodin into the shop, up early as usual, her husband a sector manager at UPS, beating the morning rush.

"Hello, Missus." Ice-packing a halved grouper.

"Hello, Fitz." Mrs. B. blotting her forehead with a handkerchief. "Boy, it's hot."

Albert runs his hands under cold water, the water feeling like fire. Wipes them with a towel. "Ginger root."

"For the heat?"

With a bone knife, slicing the sixteen ounces of fish he knows she will order. "After the cayenne pepper, you might try a little ginger root this time. On the fish. You shred it."

Albert making like he's shredding with his hands.

Terry reemerges from the back with a bucket of ice. "You can get it right over at Alfieri's," Terry says. He looks Mrs. B. over as he does every time she comes in, though she never seems to give him much of a rise.

"Alfieri's has ginger?" she asks.

Albert ringing up her fish.

"Sure they do," he says, as Terry slides the ice into the last empty bed. "They keep it in the back, in the Oriental food section. They—"

Bobby Kelly sticks his head in from the loading dock, trying to impress a new buyer, arm around her shoulder, his hair combed over, wet. "Come on you guys. Miss Deburque still hasn't got her order. Albert, step it up."

Albert keeping his eyes down, into the register drawer, making change.

Mrs. B. taking her fish from the counter.

"Ginger?" she asks.

"Root," Albert whispers, "you shred it." Albert again making like he's shredding.

"ALBERT!"

Lowering his hands to the countertop.

"Fuck off, Bobby," Mrs. B. says, winking, at Albert, as the screen door slaps behind her.

Bobby smiling, "Hey!", but angry just the same, what

with Miss Deburque on his arm.

"We'll be right on it, Bobby," Terry says, pulling the last grouper from the counter, slamming it onto the final bed of ice. Bobby recurls his arm around Miss Deburque, leads her back toward the loading dock. "They're good boys," he's saying, "you just got to keep an eye on them."

Terry tosses parsley clumps across the fish and ice, "Just think, Fitz, in a hundred years this could all be yours."

Spraying fish guts from the steel counter into the sink. Not minding the fish, the smell he was raised with. But the boredom. About once every six months, Bobby would bring him into the office to talk about his future, about giving him more responsibility. Bobby did this, he knew, out of respect for his mother and his da, and for the same reason Albert listened each time, though he knew Bobby thought he wasn't much for figures, and the truth was he wasn't.

And still, it's a steady check, and he was never much good on the boats and there's nothing much else that he can do.

"What exactly were you drinking about, anyway?" Terry asks.

A fly's bouncing off the inside glass of the open display case. Albert trying to chase it out with a towel.

"Old problems."

Terry nods. "So, what are you going to do about, you

know, your girl?" Terry flattens the fly dead against the glass with his hand.

"Eileen?"

"Yeah."

He cannot think of anything to immediately say.

"I mean how are you going to swing it with her and all? Not that you're married to her or nothing, but, you know, how you going to swing it?"

Albert tries to smile in the way he'd seen his father's friends do when they talked about women that were other than their own, to smile in a way that seemed to suggest something, though Albert never knew exactly what. "Let's just leave her out of this," he says, and then smiling he feels stupid, and he turns from Terry and wipes the fly off the case, tossing the towel into a can that leaps with flies when it hits.

Wiping his forehead with his sleeve. Pressing his forearm, for a moment, into his eyes. "But, Terry, this girl . . . "

"Well," Terry says, "seeing a girl and meeting a girl are two different things, Fitz."

Terry peels off his rubber gloves. His knuckles are tattooed. The set-up fist reads L-O-V-E. The right hook reads H-A-T-E. "You should have followed her."

Lowering his arm. He steadies himself against the counter, takes a deep breath, and feels the blackness recede, as if drawing back inside him. He wishes it would go.

"I couldn't."

"Couldn't?"

Rearranging Terry's parsley around the grouper, pulling the clusters apart, carefully, fixing them so they look nice.

"What do you mean, you couldn't?" A grin creeping across Terry's face. "Jesus, Albert, how bad were you?"

"Well—" rolling his eyes down, down toward the mooning grouper.

And they're laughing, Terry with a cold arm around Albert's neck.

HE WOULD not stay long at Jimmy Delancy's, would say he'd another delivery to make, though Jimmy would know it wasn't so, what with Albert never making a delivery before, and only making this one because it was a last minute order on account of an error by Delancy's new chef and Bobby's regular driver having left for his daytime job of sealing the oak trees in the Quarter that of late had been imploding from mites. Hundreds of years old, and suddenly whole trees would come down, crumbling as if they'd suddenly lost whatever it was that made them stand upright and live. He hadn't seen it himself, thought in fact that the guy was joking, until he'd read about it in the paper and figured it must be so.

He had oysters, bushels, bagged and boxed in the back

of the van. Delancy's new chef was meant to put in the order on Tuesdays, claimed that he had, but the oysters were special order and the chef hadn't put the call in until Wednesday, which meant he should not have had his oysters until Friday and Albert had to call special to Leeville, where they knew his father, and Bobby saying he was going to charge Delancy for the extra cost.

Driving up St. Charles, passing the streetcar he rides every morning and night, leaving the Quarter behind him. The old hotels and now the neon. He liked the older places, that seemed about to slide or topple into the street, patrons, bar tops, and all. Like those oak trees, and he eyes an oak as he comes to a red light, waiting for the tree to burst from within.

Pulling past St. Sebastian's, children at their desks. Two nuns up front, young nuns he does not recognize. It always surprises him to see nuns younger than he, though at thirty-five this was becoming more frequent.

He'd met Eileen, four years ago, at a St. Sebastian's reunion. He'd known her before, but only as a girl; she'd be in the choir when he'd be helping Father Tim, she'd been eleven when he was sixteen. At the reunion, she'd mainly hung around Sandy, but then Sandy'd introduced her to him, and he'd recognized her from the short bangs and the brown eyes that were auburn ringed. When they met, there at St. Sebastian's, four years ago, she'd just been left by the man she'd meant to marry.

Albert was her rebound. He knows that, she said as much to him. She had sloe gin in her purse and she'd been pouring it into ginger ales and behind the rectory she'd fixed him a drink and then she'd told him how the man she thought she'd loved was leaving her. Of how she did not want to drink like her mother, who drank alone, with her own man dead, and then she'd toasted his plastic cup of ginger ale and gin, and poured in more gin, toasting the cup again, and she was crying, tears from her eyes that in the light of the overcast night seemed even then quick to him, quick in a way that suggested she might show him things he did not already know.

She had, in a way. She'd shown him that the line between like and love was unclear; how she could love him but not be in love. She'd said that straight away, before Audrey was born, before Audrey even began to press out from her belly, that she could believe he'd be a good father, but that she and their child would still live alone. And now they no longer lived alone, with Hank. And he knows now that it was the drinking and his eagerness and her hurt that brought her to him, but he cannot reason how Audrey could have been born from deception and sin. Or from anything but love.

Traffic slow, so he turns past St. Sebastian's, and down along Magazine, to roll through the neighborhood, although it's a little out of the way: driving past the antique shops with the heavy wood furniture and the bums out front; the new high-priced shops squeezing in beside the cigar stores and his da's VFW and the Treetop Grocery where he'd still get a meat-loaf po'boy some Wednesdays to take in for lunch. He'd swing by and surprise his ma, but she was out with Mrs. Neil. Past the RTA bus barn. The blue gantry cranes rising from the river wharves. The train that still runs along Tchoupitoulas. And Eileen's mother, just three blocks away.

He hasn't seen Eileen's mother for two years. Eileen had wanted her to move in with a sister in Lake Charles, where, Eileen said, she could drink and gamble her way to the grave for all she cared. That was not right. Although he understood that with the therapy and the AA, Eileen had come to see that her mother had not raised her well, with the drinking. But still, she had been to St. Sebastian's, and even if the board had paid for her, and even if Eileen had cooked for herself, there had to remain some connection with those who gave you life, even if life was not always as clear as the young nuns would make it out to the children to be.

And back up, across St. Charles, down along Kerry Street, to the green neon of Delancy's Chop House, the parking lot half-full with the early uptown crowd.

Inside and the kitchen is busy with lunch. Chops and the smell of fresh mint, the bubble of thick chowder in two deep pots, the scent of sweet onion and flames leaping around panfuls of fat shrimp, the marsala wine, black pepper and thyme. Stainless blades across house-smoked salmon, a sous chef with a box of black berries. Capers in a plastic drum. And the smoke that carries so many things: the garlic and the pepper seed, steak rubbed in red wine and salt, potatoes smashed with cream, whole scoops of butter rolling toward the pan edge, bacon, sour cream and chives. He can hear Delancy's voice from his office, on the telephone, carrying through this mesh, a mesh that Albert lets hold him until the weight of the oysters pulls him toward the sink.

"Delivery," he says to Delancy's new chef, whom he doesn't know well, who's stirring a marinara that Albert can tell from the color has been cooked at slightly too high a heat.

The chef slaps the wooden spoon hard against the marinara pot's edge, turns his back, bends over to check the lowest stove.

The sous chef takes Bobby's clipboard, initials beside Jimmy Delancy's name.

"There's an extra cost."

Albert's never seen the sous chef before, must be new also, Delancy having to hire the head chef less than a month ago when Gerry Connoly left with his new wife for Houston. The sous chef says nothing, glances nervously toward the stove, then toward Jimmy Delancy's office, and quickly nods.

"God damn to hell—" And the chef's holding his burnt hand and he's kicking the stove, really kicking it, and Delancy's door swings open and Albert grabs the clipboard and makes fast for the door.

"Albert!"

Delancy there, in the sweater his ma had given him the Christmas past, somehow filling the entire doorway with himself despite his being no taller than Albert, and certainly not as wide.

"Albert, I'm just off the phone." The chef's glaring at Delancy who ignores him, Albert holding the clipboard up across his chest. "I've got you and Eileen next to me at the head table," Delancy says, "with your ma." Delancy steps into the kitchen. "So for God's sake wear a clean shirt."

Albert smiles but does not meet Delancy's eyes.

"And Albert—"

Turning his body toward the loading dock, staring into the sunlight beyond the screen. "I've got to go Jimmy. I don't normally drive the van."

"As I say, I don't know if there'll be any food at the wedding. My chef might forget to cook it. But at least there'll be a band."

The chef storms past the oysters to his office.

Albert nods, smiles quickly, and steps toward the truck. "See you, Jimmy."

But Delancy is snatching up the invoice and throwing

open the chef's closed door so that the knob swings out and slaps the wall, the door bouncing back, slamming shut, sealing Delancy inside.

JACKSON SQUARE at noontime, kids with skateboards, tourists, shoe-shine guys, painters who'll make your name into art, on a corner bench so that he can see up the alleyway, the Cathedral crosses above him. Finishing his sandwich, feeling better, a Dr. Pepper on the bench by his knee.

Glancing up the alley to the steps where she stood. He's got a right. His da always said that, that one man's got as much right as another to walk on God's earth.

He would have told his father that Eileen was with child, if his father had not been so ill. His father often spoke of grandchildren, "what's the matter with my two sons," he'd say. But Sandy didn't find Colleen until later, and Albert mostly working. His father would have been happy with the news, but this would have meant setting a date for the wedding before his father died.

Six months after his father's passing, Audrey had been born.

Crumpling the sandwich foil.

He'd tried to see Eileen, as their baby grew inside of her, with her Aunt moved in with her mother and her, but he'd felt unnecessary, not because of the women, but because Eileen seemed to need him less and less. He'd come over on a Saturday and then on the Sundays, too, as she'd stopped coming to Mass, with Father King suggesting it was because of the heat, but Albert knowing better. The pregnancy was changing her. Eileen did not want him, even as he felt a love he could not well express for the baby she carried. She'd taken birthing classes and he thought he might help her with the breathing, offered to take the Tuesday mornings off from work. But she said she did not want him to interrupt his schedule, to take the cut in pay, though a few Tuesdays did not matter much to him, and so he'd see her on Saturday nights, mostly sitting with her Aunt and her mother, the four of them watching the television.

And then she had AA and new friends and her waitressing job, and he saw her less and less, and they never did once hold hands again after their night together. Then, two years later, a year ago, in City Park, when he'd lifted Audrey off the lime-green horse, when he'd bought Audrey her first lemon sno-ball, while he'd still held Audrey's small hand, she'd told him about Hank and he saw what it was for Eileen to love.

At the park fence, a woman is painting mirror frames. As he turns, he sees himself: the red hair creeping back from his forehead, thick as brushes; the pink skin, *pink*; round face, *too* round, like the rest of him. But he is strong, his neck and arms, and he hasn't missed a work day since his da's funeral three years before.

His eyebrows are too bushy. His fingers fat and short. There's a scab on his forehead. His cheeks make him look like a boy. He turns away.

The church bells ringing, the clouds up above. Squeezing the foil into the tightest possible ball. Hurling it into the trash.

In the lobby of the Blue Royale Hotel, Albert buttoning and unbuttoning the top button at the neck of his blue windbreaker. Buttoning, a fold of flesh rides over his collar. Unbuttoning, the rising stink of fish.

He breathes in, clenches his teeth, and buttons the windbreaker fast; hurrying toward the marble reception counter, past the potted palms, avoiding the antique mirrors, eyes down at the blue and cream carpet, up at the painted ceiling that shows pink cupids and clouds.

Hand through his hair, swallowing hard, smiling at the desk clerk, a tall woman, younger than he, the floor behind the counter elevated, the clerk looking down at him, slightly.

"Deliveries in the back."

Feeling his ears flush red. "I'm not here for a delivery. I want to inquire about a guest."

"—room? A guest room?"

Eyes on the marble counter. The corners of his lips tightening and retightening, hoping his ears don't give him away.

"No, a guest. I saw her last night."

The clerk's face distorts in the marble's shine. He raises his face. Her eyes are hidden in the light of the chandelier that reflects off the thick lenses of her silver eyeglass frames. "She's tall, maybe your height, with blonde hair, a white dress."

"Sir—"

"She was driving a Jaguar. Well, she was with a man who was driving a Jaguar. She wouldn't let him kiss her."

The clerk glances past him, and Albert feels suddenly that he is lost.

"Sir, we don't keep mug shots of our guests. I cannot give out information—"

"She's my sister."

"Oh."

The Clerk glances past him again. He sees her slightly nod. She looks back at him. She smiles.

"What's her name?"

"She's just been married, see, so I don't know her name."

Looks down, then past her, back to the mirror where a man in a blazer with the hotel crest stitched to the pocket is standing beneath a painting of two red circles, looking him up, then looking him down.

"I happened to be in the neighborhood."

When a hand lands gently on his arm, he does not have to turn his head to know whose it is.

"Would you step out of line, please?"

Albert's gaze dropping, across the small space of rich carpet, from his own shoes, worn thin, cheap to begin with, to the dick's black, polished loafers, with the tassels.

"OK." He nods at the clerk. "I'm sorry." Nods at the dick. "I'm sorry."

Face hot, hurrying across the lobby, the doorman giving the revolving door a heavy push, Albert closing his eyes, breath held, pushing through, out into the thick, familiar air of the Quarter.

Riding uptown, his da's hat in his lap, his windbreaker flapping slightly in the streetcar's opened glass window. Alone on the bench seat, three nuns across from him in a seat meant for two. The sun's last gold on his hands, on his shirt front and work pants that are heavy with his sweat.

Staring straight ahead, out the driver's windshield, lips pressed tightly together.

Riding downtown, in his blue church suit, his best suit, his only suit, the streetcar crowded, carrying folks back to the Quarter for nighttime. A man in a yellow V-neck sweater sits next to him, reading a copy of the *New York Times*. Over the man's shoulder, the ad for the Pinnacle House, above a kid with a green afro, next to an ad for Pepsodent. A fly's bouncing off the hotel's pink steps, Albert wishing he had a *New York Times* or a *Times Picayune* so he could flatten it.

The doors of the Blue Royale Hotel spinning and Albert tugging on the slightly short sleeves of his suit jacket. When he tugs the right sleeve, the left shoulder bunches up. When he tugs the left sleeve, the right shoulder bunches up. Right-left, left-right, he considers turning back, rushing down the blue-lit steps, maybe crossing back to that bar and finding the old man with his stubborn ideas about gumbo.

But the doorman is swinging the door for him, creating a current that Albert steps into. Taking small steps forward, Albert sees the Quarter, where he's spent his life selling fish, reflected, spinning away from him. Stepping into the gold and cream of the lobby.

He brings his hand to his hair, to his collar, to the jacket hem, quickly to check his fly. A woman in a chair with a drink and a cheese tray coughs, her face chalk white, her hair in tight curls, older than his mother, a small dog in her lap, the fur at the dog's lips greasy with cheese. Trying to stay calm, unnoticeable in a place such as this. Smiling, worrying about the hotel dick, hoping that the sweat he feels doesn't soak through his jacket, under the arms, making him seem unclean. Eyes down, at his black shoes which he polished with navy blue because it was all that his mother had, at his feet moving suddenly fast.

Beyond any current is the place where the water is still and he feels that now, ten steps from the reception desk, realizes he could easily turn and find the stronger flow that would take him back, down the steps, into the Quarter, maybe to that bar, maybe to the river where he might walk and have a cola sno-ball—maybe even to Bobby's where he might stop in and see if Bobby was doing the books, might finally take an interest in the business side of things as his da had always urged him to do— but he keeps moving, and soon his hands are resting again on the reception's marble counter.

"Yes, sir?"

The thin, too-neat woman is gone, replaced by an even thinner, neater man.

"I—"

A couple fills the space behind him, reflected in the mirror beyond the counter, through a vase of dried, flowerless twigs. The woman's in a red dress, the man's in a tuxedo. The mirror is gold, the chandelier crystal, the pen near Albert's hand is silver and it shines.

"Sir, can I help you?"

"I—"

He feels the clerk's eyes on him. Then past him, and he sees the slight nod that's returned in the mirror by the couple.

"I—".

"We just want an extra key," says the man in the tuxedo.

He steps quickly aside.

The way the woman slips her bare arm into the space between the man's biceps and side. The way the man leads her, without effort, key in his pants' pocket, gliding toward the Blue Royale Room.

And past them in the restaurant's foyer, she is suddenly there. Green eyes, from even that distance; hair a crown of light.

A towering spray of flowers; rising, rising, the domed, gold ceiling in clouds above her head.

"Yes, sir, now what were we going to help you with?"

But he is halfway to her.

She is turning away, joining the couple, and the space between him and her is as if elastic, his feet barely gaining the ground, and he feels for a moment his legs as when he'd carried his father's casket, time slow and then suddenly fast, his da at once in the ground, and when he reaches the foyer she is gone. Alone, a fat cupid floats in the domed foyer ceiling.

He pulls in his belly, hikes up the waistline of his pants. Looks down at his shoes. The toe's already scuffed, the polish not sticking to the front tip of the thin sole that's worn grey. He shifts a little to his left, shuffling his feet, hiding his toes beneath the blue linen tablecloth that drapes the mahogany table that holds the flowers that rise up the dark wood wall.

Alone, not wanting to look expectant, not wanting to

look out of place; hearing her laughter from the bar where she's joined the couple, just beyond where he can see, wondering how he will meet her. Picking a white rose from the spray, twirling it in his hands.

Thinking. The Royale Room: dark wood tables, pale-blue tableclothes, the mahogany bar that catches the city lights from the window that runs the length of the restaurant, the window revealing the Quarter, reflecting a trio playing low in the dining room's corner.

A streetcar beyond the window. Watching it trail down its tracks, the red lights blending and then disappearing into the night.

The trio's drummer coughs and picks up his brushes, the band into a standard he doesn't know. He finds her again, she in a white linen blouse, straight olive pants, flat shoes because she's tall, taller than him; leaning across two businessmen in suits, one touching her arm, the other laughing in a way Albert does not like at something she has said.

Pressed near the foyer wall, shuffling slightly from foot to foot, he forces himself to stop. Her smile makes him feel his stomach's center; he presses a hand to his belly. Pulls it in. She turns from the two men, tugs a little at the front of her blouse, smoothing, the V at her neckline deepening, a flat gold chain against her skin.

She heads straight at him.

He swallows twice, forces his shoulders back, standing straighter. This would be his chance. Look casual. Puts a hand on the wall. Worries about his sweat, lowers it. Brings it fast to his hair. The rose digs in. Shoves the stem back into the arrangement, shakes his hair quickly for the petals. Looks around, slaps his hands behind him, lifts his chin, belly back, deep breath, and smile. Hoping to appear relaxed.

"Hello," to him and she's smiling, arriving, her teeth as white as sugar.

"Huh-huh," he says. Closing his eyes, quickly, thinking to clear his throat. "Hello."

Glancing at the life in her smile. Not daring to meet her eyes. Giving a last hack so she doesn't think he's an idiot.

"Just one?" she asks.

"Yes," he says. Then, because he's not sure what she means, to cover things, he looks up, "No."

Smiling.

She smiles back.

Smiling wider.

She picks up a menu.

He steps out from behind the foyer table. "Oh, sure, yes, just me."

He takes a breath. Following. He likes the way she walks. Tall, upright, like a strong sail. He lets his eyes linger at the drape of the shirt at her hips.

She turns, a blonde curl falls across her green eyes. His ears hot.

"Business?"

Too quickly, "Fish!"

"Fish?"

Feeling the sweat beneath the broadcloth of his suit. "I love it."

He claps his hands.

"Well, good." That smile again. "We have a very fresh grouper tonight. Enjoy yourself."

Pulling out the chair at his table. She does not wear a ring. He sits.

A table in the window, with the city as the backdrop. He recognizes the new insurance tower with its silver dome, above the department store with the doorman and the valet that they had to tear down LeRouix Market and Fantail Bakery and Alligator Gifts to build.

He turns back to see her gone. He watches her steering among the tables, smiling, the saxophone player giving a little vibrato as she passes.

Albert shuts his eyes and still sees that smile. He inhales, tries to draw her in, remembering her scent, trying to save it in his body, trying to replace the thickness in his guts with her smell. And then she's out of view in the foyer and he feels the eyes of the couple on him from the bar, though when he glances at them they've already looked away. He looks down to the table. The menu laid out between columns of cutlery.

So she worked in the restaurant, she was not a guest. He did not care: it was a place like he had never seen, with the carpet thick and the marble-top bar and the trio and the city beyond him. And the grace is hers, her smile, the way her laughter filled him with a lightness, and he can see his ma laughing with her, at the Sunday dinners, with his brother and the Father there, and Jimmy Delancy, Albert sitting in his da's old chair, holding onto her hand.

He straightens the knife. Touches the base of the spoon. He would not get ahead of himself. He'd gotten ahead of himself before with Eileen, had not listened, he knew now, to her real feelings. Things had started well enough with Eileen, after he'd called her from Bobby's, getting her phone number from Sandy who'd got it for him from Father King. She'd cooked for him on their first date, spaghetti with meatballs made from hot sausage. They'd had a walk down Magazine, after their first dinner, the mother asleep in a chair, out from the drink, and he promised to walk with her along the river, where he'd brought bread for the gulls, and she'd promised to make him dinner again when her mother went to visit her aunt and it was that day, in Eileen's girlhood bed, just a week after meeting her at the St. Sebastian's reunion, with the clovers on the bedspread and a newspaper photo of five girls playing tennis that she'd torn out as a girl, beneath two paint-by-numbers pictures of horses in blue-green fields, with the wine bottle rolling off the side table to land with a thick pop across the pile of their clothing, there they had come together, at thirty-two years old, with Eileen drunk, and Albert hoping that this was what love was.

He's made a fingerprint on the spoon. He wipes it. Takes a sip of water. His hands are shaky. He picks up the menu so that its bottom edge rests steadily on the blue cloth, and he opens it. He scans the entrees, the prices, his cheeks puffing out, coughs, sips a little more water, glances again to see who's watching him, nods, then sets the menu carefully aside.

Later and the trio's slowed. The half-eaten grouper sits cold on his plate. The lights of the French Quarter behind him, the hush of conversation, and Albert staring across the dining room, watching her.

She's been busy all night. It was something, the way she moved among all these people, the way she laughed like music, how she smiled at so many things. She was so light. He could almost see her thin ankles lifting her feet off the carpet. He'd hoped she'd come by the table and ask if he needed anything, but she hadn't.

When she looks up from her reservation book, he quickly looks away.

A woman's laughter.

Crimson and heat through his face.

The Quarter lights, a sax wail, the spray of flowers. Albert glares into his cold fish, into the reflection of his face in the porcelain beneath. He throws his napkin across it.

Shoving the plate away—rising, pushing up from the table, water slopping from its glass. A man has a right.

Breathing in, out, Albert, at the trio, thirty feet from her; at the bar, twenty feet; at the foyer edge, ten.

He slows.

He smoothes his jacket, runs a hand two times through his hair.

The music picks up, the bass challenging the saxophone and the drum.

He steps toward her.

The Jag man enters from the hotel's lobby cutting a diagonal across Albert's path such that all Albert can do is turn like a hook and pretend to be studying the glassed-in wines that fill a case at the entrance to the foyer.

The Jag man's voice is quick and pinched. He's in a blue suit like Albert's, only the Jag man's is lighter and it fits.

" . . . two tickets . . ."

Albert focuses his ears.

" . . . two tickets for Johnny Niles, Chelsea."

Chelsea.

Chelsea. His lips reflect back from the glass.

Chelsea.

Chelsea, like springtime. Chelsea like a fresh breeze.

Chelsea.

"Hello, Robert."

The Jag man cups her cheek, directing her face to his. *"Johnny Niles*, Chelsea."

She pulls away from his touch. "Look, Robert, you're a nice man, but I don't go out with married men, even nice ones."

She tries to focus on her ledger.

"I thought we talked about that last night."

Watching the Jag man slide his hand to Chelsea's shoulder, watching him finger the narrow shirt collar of her white blouse.

"I'm back down from Manhattan on Tuesday. They're front row seats." He runs his hand to the skin of her neck. "You should relax, Chelsea."

The Jag man leans in and presses his lips to her cheek.

"Let yourself have some fun."

She smiles thinly, nods, quickly makes for the dining room, passing Albert without a glance. The Jag man's eyes meet Albert's in the reflection of the wine case. Albert looks away, turns, nods slightly, feeling dizzy, feeling suddenly like he might be sick, stuck between the table and the spinning hotel doors.

HE COMES IN the Fitzmorris front door, the trip from the hotel foyer to his front room one of blackness, pressing at once down and also up, a dark pressure in his stomach and bowels, a spinning in his head.

His ma there, gluing yarn trunks onto felt elephants for

the nursery school class she still teaches twice a week at St. Sebastian's. In front of the color TV, waiting for the nightly weather.

"Did you and Eileen have a nice time?"

He stands in the shadows between the front room and the kitchen, his bedroom door open behind him.

"Sure, Ma," he says and he moves toward it.

Pulling his necktie from his shirt collar, draping it over his shoulder.

"Night, Ma."

He moves along the dark edge of the kitchen, closing shut his bedroom door.

He strips off his jacket. Pulls his white shirt over his head and hangs it on the chair that Sandy'd left when he'd moved. His dress shoes he returns to the back wall of his closet, behind his work shoes and his sneakers. Pulls off his belt. Steps from his pants, belly over briefs, pink between the band of his shorts and the bottom of his undershirt.

A cross above the bed. The mirror over the dresser hung with his St. Christopher medal. Tucked in the mirror frame, a black-and-white photo of his da in 1944, a boatswain's mate fighting the War. And the color snapshot of Audrey in her pink dress in front of the spinning carousel, Audrey just two, and Eileen out of frame, sitting beneath the live oak, on a thick root, her knees pulled up to her chest.

When Audrey was just over one, Eileen'd called him after midnight and his ma had answered because for a year after his da's death she did not sleep except in fits, and Albert taking the phone and Eileen saying she wanted them to do something together, as a family of three. And quickly, they were doing things together, more than they ever had: pushing the stroller through Audubon Park, streetcar rides for sno-balls, a trip to the Jean Lafitte Swamps where Audrey saw her first snake and Albert saw an alligator, a tour of the Superdome, but it was never as he imagined it would be for those who were dating; when he saw the alligator he'd turned to tell Eileen, but she was twenty feet away, her back to him, staring across a wetland of iris. And now she was with Hank.

Lowering his torso to the bed. A forearm across his face, a hand to his belly.

The spin of the carousel. Audrey in his arms, on the lime-green pony, Eileen watching them come round, spinning past her, up and then falling away. Audrey waving, auburn hair in her eyes and across her face, her heart fast in his arms.

2

Albert walking quickly through the busy lunchtime streets. Quarter shops of all types, spilling out onto the sidewalk: muffulettas, po'boys, beignets, tobacco, peppers, sex toys. Music out opened doorways; flies pouring in.

Turning up St. Louis, passing an old harmonica player, finding the cracked paint sign of the barely dressed cabaret singer carrying a pizza pie. Izzy's Pizza Cabaret.

Winding through the tables of the crumbling, turn-of-the-century dry-fish warehouse, the tables tight with students, tourists, young businessmen. Past a red-curtained stage for the nightly shows. He's never been. They're fun, Eileen assured him.

Peering through the swinging steel doors.

Pizzas up in the air, vegetables chopping, meat smoking in big pans, pop music clanging from a portable stereo on a shelf. Waitresses in short skirts and tight shirts sliding pies onto big trays, cheese clinging to the racks. He finds Eileen, her hands moving everywhere as she speaks, cracking up a group of waitresses.

He smoothes his hair, almost despite himself, and pushes through the swinging doors.

Eileen burns her finger on the pizza rack as Albert touches her shoulder. "Ah, shit! Al, hi."

She sucks on the burn.

"She's in the back."

Albert nods, smiles.

The waitresses glance at each other. One of them leads the others away.

"You OK?" Albert says when they are alone.

Eileen hoists the pizza tray to her shoulder. She wiggles her finger at the edge of the tray, examining it. "I'll live."

He likes the way she wiggles her finger. He notices again, for a moment, her eyes.

"No, I mean, you know, with things."

"Sure. Things are good. Hank got me a gig at Shadowlands. I'm going to sing, Albert!" She puffs a bang from her brow.

The chef says, "*Eileen.*"

"Oh, jeez," Eileen says, "see you, Al."

He tries to smile.

"So, she's in the back?"

But it is hard when she mentions Hank.

She hurries the pizza toward the kitchen door. "Have her back by two, OK, Albert? Hank's taking her to his rehearsal. She wants a trumpet for her birthday. Can you believe that?"

The steel doors swing closed behind her, at him, then back away, at him again, and then they are still.

• • •

Moving along the stainless counter. Past the pizzas and the chefs, the smell of garlic. Onions and pepper hot in a pan. Some scallops in butter, and a doughy calzone coming out the oven red. A chef slicing mushrooms, the soft tap of the blade on the board, the chef popping the last cap straight into his mouth.

He smiles.

She is cross-legged on a tomato crate, swirling her Madeline doll around the inside of a great Pyrex bowl. He sees her before she sees him.

"Hey—"

Audrey looks up. "I'm making Madeline swim like a fish." Her red hair is his, her freckles; round cheeks beneath dark eyes that leap from her face.

The smile deep now across his cheeks. "You ready for our date?" Standing a few feet from her, wanting to press her round cheeks to his own.

"Hank's going to take me to rehearsal, Daddy."

"That's great, darling, just great."

She's leading him into the Aquarium of the Americas that's shaped like a giant wave. He's had her hand but now she is ahead of him, and he is excited too, liked the aquarium, is glad she did, despite his spending all day with fish, and he does not know if she's dropped his hand for the doors or because she did not want to hold it.

"And do sharks eat people?" she's asking, Albert reaching for the money in his wallet, Audrey already through the gates and in.

"Sure they do," he's saying, getting a dollar back for his two tens. "They do it all the time."

Her hands flat against the green glass of the enormous fish tunnel that forms the aquarium's center, fish swimming even up over their heads. Watching her eyes, her eyes following fish. Hammerheads, eels, giant angelfish gliding by.

She seems happy watching the fish, those eyes that are his mother's and Eileen's, the small hands that have so quickly grown. Hank is good to Audrey, at least he knows that. He knew that Hank took her with him to the places he'd go, that he'd rigged a stroller up to his racing bicycle and rode her around Louis Armstrong Park on the weekends. He wondered if she was used to Hank, and he thinks of how she dropped his hand, and her wanting a trumpet, and he sees them at Hank's rehearsal, Audrey in Hank's lap as he practiced, or maybe beating a drum.

Beside her, a man in a UNO sweatshirt's got his grandson up on his shoulders and the boy's laughing, bouncing his heels against his grandfather's chest. "Tuna," the grandfather says, and the boy curls over the old man's head so that their faces are joined in the glass.

"Look, Audrey," Albert says quickly, "There's a tuna."

He puts his hands on his knees so that his face is closer to hers.

"Now, that one must be a baby. Some of them tunas can grow bigger than you are, Audrey, bigger than a car even." He spreads his arms wide to indicate the length. "Too big though and you can't barely cut them; use them for cat food, not for steaks." He smiles at her. Audrey nods. For a moment he can think of nothing more to say.

Audrey taps at an eel that's sliding past. "Snake?"

"No, that's an eel!" He puts a hand on her shoulder. "Now a lot of folks call the eel a garbage fish, but the Japanese, they prize an eel. They'll eat it raw, straight from the water. Maybe with a little green mustard."

He gives her shoulder a squeeze.

"You like fish, hey, Aud?"

"Crabbies!" And she's running up a rampway.

After her, he lets her run, to a kid-sized tide pool displaying all sorts of sealife beneath a sign that reads, "Please Touch."

She's dipping her fingers into the water, drawing them quickly back. "*Star*fish."

Albert reaches in and pulls the starfish from its rock.

"He's a beauty."

Audrey brushes it with her finger.

He counts the starfish's limbs. "One two three four five." He looks up. Madeline sails across the shallow pool. "Hey!"

"She's swimming!"

He hurries Madeline from the pool before it sinks.

Shakes some water off the doll, hands the soggy Madeline back to her. Audrey presses the doll to her cheek, laughing at the wet. He shakes his head, which causes her to laugh more.

He reaches into the pool, and pulls her up a harmless crab. "Look here."

"Crabbie!"

The crab's thin legs snap in the air. He notices the eggs along its belly.

"Now, this crab is about to have babies. See this pouch? Soon it will split open and a whole bunch of little crabs will come crawling right on out."

Audrey's brow tightens. He gently sets the crab back in the water. "You can learn a lot in a place like this, hey Aud?"

Reaching down, kissing her on her cheek, and then when she offers him Madeline, kissing the wet doll as well.

On one of the wrought-iron balconies hanging over Decatur Street, Albert and Audrey, beneath a big white umbrella, waiting on lunch. He took her for the view of the river.

"Lots of people don't know how good they are," he's saying, "they got more protein than baloney or steak. People think they cost a lot, but that's just in the fancy restaurants."

Audrey's got her eyes down to a policeman on a horse that's being petted by a girl holding a big balloon. Albert watching her, making a mental note.

"We'll get a balloon after lunch, hey, Aud? One of them metal ones with stars on it or something."

A waiter in a T-shirt with the name of the restaurant spelled out across the front carries their two porcelain platters to the table.

"Lunch," Albert announces and sees her smile. Feeling the sun now and the air. Her eyes widen as the waiter lowers the two big platters to the table: soft-shell crab sandwiches, crab legs dangling out the edges of the bread.

Feeling like he could eat both sandwiches, Albert says "Dig in—" and then he does. He's two bites from the middle when he glances up. She's staring into her sandwich, Madeline looking back at him in a way that makes him uneasy.

"Crabbies," he says.

Audrey staring up at him. A crab leg disappears between his lips. She looks back down at her sandwich, her face as white as the platter.

SUN LOW OVER the Quarter, bouncing in off the empty fish beds that Terry sprays down with a hose. A radio program's arguing about whether to bring major league baseball to the city. A woman with a red scarf around her neck is looking over the few cuts of fish that weren't sold before lunch.

"You got any fresh catfish?" the woman asks.

"Everything we got is out."

Terry yells over his shoulder.

"Hey, Al, we don't got any catfish back there do we?"

Albert, in the walk-in freezer, holds his hand over the mouthpiece of the cordless phone he's got tucked between his shoulder and his chin.

Calls out to Terry, "I'm checking—" then suddenly into the phone, "yes, hello?"

Albert curls over the cordless telephone. "May I speak with Chelsea, please?" He glances out toward the front room. "Yes," he whispers. "Oh, I see. Yes. I'll try back later."

He shuts off the phone, presses his lips tight, stands for a moment alone amidst the frozen fish.

Terry sticks his head through the plastic insulating strips that hang down the cooler's entrance. "No luck?"

He studies Albert for a minute.

"You hot or something, Al?"

THE QUARTER IS lit up for nighttime—music and food and laughter, car horns, bartering, the clop-clop of hooves. Spotlights up the Cathedral—spiring the humid sky.

Albert, alone, in his blue suit, thinking, on the park bench, the wet grass dampening his Sunday shoes.

Then up, swallowing hard, at the phone kiosk, beside the fateful bar. Coins flat in his hand, two dimes in the slot, his back to the Blue Royale's entranceway across the damp stone street.

Huddled, waiting.

The receiver clicks. He grips it.

"Blue Royale room, this is Chelsea."

"Ah, hi, I—" he says, rasping, losing the courage of his voice.

A pause.

"Hello?"

Pressing the receiver to his chest. He feels his heart quickening, feels a thickness filling his belly's pit, pressing outward.

Clears his throat, fast. Spits. Looks around to make sure no one saw him spitting; brings the phone back to his lips, moistens them with his tongue

"Hello." His voice lower than usual.

"Yes?"

"This is Albert." Shutting his eyes against the stupidity.

"Who?"

Opening one eye, squinting into the cracked green paint of the phone kiosk, penciled numbers suggesting who to call for a good time; a sticker has a woman with her legs spread, a black triangle between her thighs.

"I had a nice dinner last night."

"Oh . . . good . . . are you coming in tonight?"

Moving his eyes from the phone numbers, from the

woman with the cartoon legs, to the lights of the Cathedral. The lit clouds whip above it, making it seem to fall away.

"That's what I wanted to talk to you about."

"Fine," Chelsea says. "We're not too crowded. What time is good for you? Eight-thirty all right?"

Snapping his eyes back to the phone, flustered, hand fast through his hair. "Sure, I—"

"All right, Mr. Albert, we'll see you at eight-thirty."

"Well—"

Closing his eyes, opening them.

"Thank you," he says, as the receiver clicks off.

A guy no older than him shuffles drunkenly out the bar. The guy looks once to his right, then turns to his left, and walks away, singing. Albert turns from the man, like he might be the devil himself.

In front of the big spray of flowers, hands clasped at his waist, red necktie because before he'd worn blue, swaying from foot to foot.

Waiting.

Chelsea in her white dress, a slit revealing her thighs. The necklace flat and gold along the angles of her throat.

She's on the reception telephone, telling someone that she has to go, and her face is suddenly tight, and her free hand is pressing her hair behind her ears and she is trying to get a word in but the party on the other end won't let her. Finally she says, and Albert hears this clearly, "I just have to go," and while she does not slam the receiver down, he can tell by the way she closes her eyes and breathes out fully that she has been upset. He guesses it is the man from the Jaguar and he feels an anger rise up from inside of his chest.

And he feels at once protective of her, and then she is approaching and the anger turns to fear and heat, his throat feeling thick inside its collar.

He holds his ground. Only a quick glance behind him, even as his whole body's yelling now *escape*.

"Good evening," she says.

Into her eyes, speechless. His lips a smile.

"Mr.—"

"Albert," he says.

"Mr. Albert."

"Just Albert." Smile bigger, eyebrows involved, arched up like full sails.

"Oh, I see. Same table as last night, Albert?"

"Surely." He shuts his eyes. Ask her. Opens them. "That would be fine."

Chelsea leads him across the dining room. Feeling the heavy stick of his undershirt and his shorts.

"No grouper tonight, but we've got a great filet."

Same trio, same bar.

Heading toward the same table.

They pass an old couple. The wife, reaching for her dinner roll, knocks her reading glasses to the carpet. She leans for them, her necklace dangling, the floor a long way from her chair. He picks up the eyeglasses, sets them beside the old woman's plate. The husband raises his hand in a half-salute. Chelsea's pulling out the same chair he couldn't afford to sit in the night before.

He will not sit down. Standing at the table, watching her reflected in the window glass.

"They say it may storm," he finally says.

"That'll be nice."

"Yes."

Nodding. The Quarter lights blinking within and around her.

In the foyer a couple waits to be seated. Her hand on the back of his chair.

"You like storms, too?" he asks.

She picks up his napkin.

He smiles, hovers for a moment, then sits. She drapes the napkin across his lap, too quickly he thinks, like she wants to go.

He looks at her. She's watching a couple seated nearer the bar. The man in a black suit, the woman, much younger, in a tight silver dress.

"Enjoy your dinner, Albert."

And she moves away.

Albert slowly rising, catching the napkin before it slides to the ground.

"Excuse me." Too loudly.

The old couple glances over. Chelsea turns.

"Yes?"

The sweat is outside of his clothes now, he can feel it along his hairline, curling down toward his eyes.

"I was wondering."

Fidgeting with the napkin.

"That is if you're free and all."

He glances quickly around the room, swallows hard, nearly whispers. "Would you like to have dinner with me, Chelsea?"

A sweat bead has reached the tip of his nose and he knows she can see it and he needs to wipe it but he doesn't want to be wiping his fat nose at a time like this and then his ears that were red to begin with begin to burn and with the burning and the itching he almost does not hear her say, "Sure, Albert, I'll have dinner with you."

She's watching the girl at the bar, who looks bored, but the girl's laughing, and he sees Chelsea's face in profile, the light from the tables darkening one side, and he feels a rising fear.

"Sure? Oh," he says, bringing the napkin to his forehead. "Fine." He sinks woozily into his chair.

"Give me your number when you leave tonight."

And he's rising again, as if pulled by those eyes. "May I give it to you now, ha-ha?" He pats his belly. "I'm actually, ha!, trying to lose a little weight." Grinning.

The girl's letting the man cover her hands in his, and

the man does not stop talking, as if he's done this his whole life, and Chelsea says, "All right," and when she turns again she seems far away and then she smiles and he feels her near to him once more.

They head back across the dining room, Albert still clutching his napkin. The old lady shoots him a little congratulatory nod. Chelsea seems light again and she smiles.

"I don't think you need to lose weight," Chelsea says.

"Really?"

As the saxophone leaps into a lead.

ALBERT, DRUMMING a beat against the painted steel railing that separates the Quarter from the riverbank. Drumming and drinking a Dr. Pepper, it tasting like nectar. Riverboats gliding by. Lovers crowding the flat-stone bank, drinking liquor from paper cups, some with their shoes kicked off, snuggling against the river's breeze.

The Mississippi, fifteen feet above the city which, to keep from drowning, is criss-crossed with levees, spillways and canals.

And Albert, the moon up above, the slap of the water against the stones, finishing his Dr. Pepper, lowering the empty can to the rail. He can see them there, along the river, the lights of the boats and the city, the warmth of her across him.

A police siren from Decatur. A bottle rolls along the rocks. He gives the empty can a shake. And he does up his jacket, what with that breeze, and turns his back to the river. Staring into the Quarter, trying to warm himself, trying to remember how warm he was feeling just moments ago.

MORNING. HUMMING, pouring whipped eggs into a hot iron skillet, his white apron swaying at his hips.

Singing, "*Sweet Car-o-line*," Neil Diamond, his father's favorite, his da'd play it mornings from the cassette player beside the sink.

Sliding tomatoes and green peppers into the eggs, folding the omelet, his eyebrows raising up as he lifts, down as he lowers and folds. He gives the pan a couple of taps, flips the spatula in the air.

At the kitchen table, his ma's spoon is frozen midway between her corn flakes and her mouth.

"Reaching out, touching me—"

Sliding the omelet onto his mother's empty plate.

"*Touching you*—" He raps her plate a couple times with his spoon. "There we are, Ma. Just like da used to make it." Folds a paper napkin across her lap, kisses her on the cheek. "More coffee?"

She slams her hands to the wooden table. "That does it! What's going on?"

Smiling a little, "Ma?" Giving her innocent blue eyes.

His ma grinning, "All right for you." She reaches out and pinches him. "But just remember, your mother knows everything."

She cuts into the omelet.

"Listen, Al, I was at the school yesterday and Sister Cady still says it would be no problem to get Audrey in for October, despite the waiting list."

He eats his omelet standing up, in four big bites. Stacks the plate on top of the pan in the sink, opens the refrigerator, pulls out an aluminum bowl.

"If she was in the Tuesday-Thursday group, I'd get to see her every week."

He draws in a breath. "She's going to the Montessori in January. In the Faubourg-Marigny. I've told you before, Ma. That's what Eileen wants."

"She's Catholic."

"She is."

"And how will she pay for it?"

"Ma, I'll take care of it, all right?" He sets the bowl hard to the counter. He turns down the player. "I don't want to talk anymore about Audrey's school. I'm not the only one with a say in it."

He feels the rim of the bowl dig into his palms.

"Albert—"

"I'll take care of it." He realizes he's spoken too loud. "I'll take care of everything."

She's got out her canvas teaching bag and she's pushed the omelet away.

He pulls the strips of marinated salmon from the metal bowl, lays them into a glass baking pan, soaking the bowl in the sink. "I just got things on my mind." The tape clicks over to the side with the Irish ballads. *Carrickfergus*.

She used to sing it sometimes around the house.

With a black magic marker she's labeling cardboard stars with her students' names. Once a year, on the Monday before Fat Tuesday, she brings her St. Sebastian's kids to the house, with the senior teachers and the nuns and lately Father King, and they sing songs and have king cakes and fruit punch and she'll allow the sisters just one Hail Mary apiece.

"Will you make the poker game this afternoon?"

"I've gone to every game for the three years now."

"That's nice."

He hates for her to worry.

"Sorry, Ma."

"Don't let Mr. Neil swindle you."

The squeak of the marker on the stars.

"That little man took your father every Saturday for forty years."

He sprinkles the salmon with a mixture of herbs he'd bought fresh from Alfieri. "Thanks for the tip, Sharky."

Sniffs it. Rinses his hands, the St. Sebastian's dishrag, pulls on his windbreaker and his da's black hat. "Will you get some more eggs, Ma? I'm going to make Audrey a cake."

He leans in and kisses her.

"Watch him if he takes four cards!"

He likes the way her brown eyes open wide when she's happy, morning glories his da used to say, and he thinks of Chelsea's eyes, the silver around the green, the way she'd touched his arm when she'd given him her phone number, the way she smiled and the courtesy she'd shown in not making him order a meal when he didn't feel like it, and he kisses his ma again.

"Don't forget about St. Sebastian's."

"All right, Ma." Staring into the blue stars.

BACK IN THE KITCHEN of Delancy's Chop House, only this time he's warming what he's brought, the door wide open to the card room where the old men are playing a hand without him. Sitting around the whiskey-filled table as they have every Saturday for forty years.

He hears Jimmy Delancy, the same age as his father if his father had lived, a White Owl bobbing up and down between his lips; he knows Delancy is frowning at his cards. "Well, I'm up the Pope's ass without a paddle," Delancy says, his voice carrying into the kitchen and, Albert imagines, out into the street as well.

"Please Jimmy," says Father King, who'd taken the seat from Father Tim in 1974.

An eye on the game, an eye on the kitchen around him. Alone but for the chef's assistant who's chopping up potatoes for Delancy's famous smashed. The stove is stainless steel, two ovens the size of fish cases, the steel scrubbed, the eight burners giving an even flame which he knows because he'd turned them on when the assistant chef wasn't looking. Above it the big pans, heavy, seasoned iron; and the display of sharp knives with their wood handles worn from use. In the walk-in fridge, the whole salmons and chops on wax paper, and another cooler just for desserts.

He watches Father King glance nervously, suspiciously, across and down, at Elliot Neil who's whispering something to Topper O'Brien, the oldest at eighty-four, Topper not understanding Neil because, as his da had put it, he's deaf as sod. When his father passed, Albert assumed his father's seat, and he's played every Saturday now for the three and a half years.

Wiping his hands on a towel. As a boy, they'd eat at the Chop House on special occasions, when his father might have a good season, before the Gulf became lifeless, or on his ma's birthday, and Delancy would bring him and Sandy into the kitchen, Sandy talking with Mrs. McCabe who'd give them mints, and Albert with Gerry Connolly, the chef, who might show him flat crates of strawberries, to be stuffed into ice cream, coated with brown sugar, burned with a butane torch and served to Albert in a bowl before he even had his dinner.

Father King lights a Pall Mall from the short end of the

one that's already lit in his mouth. The Father cautiously pushes three red chips to the pot at the center of the table. "I'll raise seventy-five," Father King says. Elliot Neil shifts a card from the right side of his hand to the left. Then back again.

When he'd first taken his father's chair, in the poker room, between Topper O'Brien and Elliot Neil, with the photographs of boxers and cowboys and riverboats, with Huey Long hung upside down and the Blessed Mother on a wall to herself, the games became quiet. He'd been to some Saturdays when he was a kid, his da wanting him, his da said, to see something other than sewing circles and crosses. He'd fetch whiskey and ashtrays for the men, eating the sandwiches Delancy would have made and set on a tray. On a few occasions, his father would ask him which card to play, or whether he should hold or fold, and on those occasions Albert would climb into his father's lap, even when he was ten, and feel good in the heat of his father's skin, the smell of whiskey on his da's breath, the scruff of his Saturday beard against Albert's smooth face. Mostly, his father was silent, and mainly Albert spent Saturdays with the sisters at St. Sebastian's, preparing for Sunday, and when he was twelve Bobby Kelly had taken him on, paying him out of his pocket.

The kitchen timer dings. Glancing at the clock, opening the oven door. Normally, he would not use a timer, but with the assistant there, he didn't want to suggest that he didn't know what he was doing, or that he was wasting gas, and have the assistant tell the new chef. He opens the oven. He breathes in the hot smell of salmon and lemon and garlic and thyme, with hot pepper flake, and hoisin also from Alfieri's, and ginger shredded across the top like cheese.

Pops a salmon round into his mouth. Eyes shoot open. Fast to the sink, mouth beneath the tap. Looks up, the assistant chef eyeing him. Grabs a towel. Wiping dry the counter, wiping dry the sink, the faucets, quickly picking up his tray, nodding, stepping back into the game room where Elliot Neil's still considering his cards.

And considering them.

And—

"Oh, for God's sake," Delancy moans.

—considering them.

"Will you hurry it up, Elliot?" Delancy says. "Topper here doesn't have many years left in him."

Topper O'Brien smiles, takes a little whiskey.

Elliot Neil collapses his cards together, presses the single exposed card tightly to his chest. "All right, then," Neil says, as if he's just been called to testify against his own ma, "I'll see the seventy-five cents. Call."

Father King inhales deeply. Holding the smoke in his lungs, the Father lays down his cards: Queens and sevens.

Three aces.

The smoke rushes out of the priest. "Oh, Elliot!"

Delancy and Topper O'Brien heaving with laughter,

Elliot Neil nodding faster now, gathering up the chips, the Father slumping his head to his hands.

"Three aces and he hesitates," says Delancy, relighting his White Owl. "Three aces! The man is a model of hesitation. No wonder you only got three kids, Elliot."

Elliot Neil pools the winnings into his grand stash. "But eleven grandchildren."

The men smile.

Delancy nodding, "Fair play to you. But I'll be catching you soon. Isn't that right, King?"

"God willing," says Father King.

"Here you go, guys." He steps into the room, tightly holding the tray of salmon in front of him, so he doesn't drop it like he once did with a forty pound wahoo that landed straight onto Bobby Kelly's foot.

Delancy tamps out his cigar. "You didn't get in the way of the chef, did you?"

"I slipped them in and out of the oven." Albert sets a plate to the side of each old man.

"Good. 'Cause he's become a royal pain in the ass."

Delancy takes two, then three salmon toasts, passes the tray to Father King. Albert takes his place in the empty chair between Topper and Father King, the men chomping into their food.

"These are delicious, Albert," Father King says. "What are they?"

"Salmon, mostly," Albert says.

Elliot Neil nods appreciatively, holds the little sand-wich out in front of him, tipping his head back and look-ing down the lower third of his thick lenses to inspect it. "What's this, paprika?" Neil asks.

"Ginger root," Albert says. "And a little fresh horseradish."

Topper grins, his teeth, like his hearing, not what they once were. "Very nice, Albert."

Albert smiles.

Delancy relights his cigar. "Ladies, can we play cards? Neil here needs to be in bed by seven-thirty."

Elliot Neil frowns. "Forty years, the same jokes."

Albert speaks into Topper's good ear, "You need me to deal for you, Topper?"

Topper nods, raises his clawed fingers. "These damn hands."

Albert deals. He hasn't much to say at the games, mainly speaking when spoken to. Most days, he's asked about business at Bobby's and about his ma, and hears stories about his mother being a saint, or the days when his da and Delancy were in the merchant marine. Once, early on, he won twenty dollars and Delancy had called him a sandbagger, but mainly if he won or lost it was closer to five. As the last card hits the table, he figures he has pretty average luck, though maybe it's changing lately for the better.

Delancy pours Jameson for those who need it, mainly for Topper and himself.

Gathering up his cards.

Father King says, "Two more weeks, Jimmy," and Albert sees Delancy stiffen.

"Don't say it, Father," Delancy says. "My Kara's marrying a good man and all, but, oh, how I wish it were done with. My daughter's wedding was less struggle than my granddaughter's is turning out to be." Delancy tosses a couple cards face down on the table. "Two, Albert."

He deals Delancy two cards.

"Two, also, for me, Albert," Topper says.

Deals Topper two cards, glances at Father King.

Father King, a cigarette like a rod from his lips, says, "Hold."

They look to Elliot Neil. Elliot Neil sorts, then resorts his cards. Albert does not want to interrupt his father's friend, and the other men don't prompt him. Neil sorting in the way that used to drive his father mad. Albert remembering the way his father would get redder and redder as Mr. Neil sorted card after card until his hand appeared to Albert to be back to where it started. When Albert'd taken up his father's place in the game, when his da was sick and insistent, when his ma said that if that's what his father wanted then it should be done, and Albert not minding, he knew the rules, and understanding how Sandy couldn't be expected to go what with a wife, though he at that time had Eileen with Audrey on the way, when he'd taken his father's own seat, Albert would report back to his da Elliot Neil's various moves and for the moment the color would come back to his da's pale skin.

And seeing. Morphine needles, the IV pouch, his mother praying in his da's leather chair; coming home on the night that Eileen said she'd raise their child alone, to find his ma with the TV on, with the Bible open to John, with his father in Sandy's old bed, the men at this table having taken up a collection so that he could die in peace at home.

His name coming through. And finding a salmon toast just outside his mouth, he bites into it. Deals Elliot Neil the four cards he'd somewhere heard him ask for. On the fourth card he remembers what his mother said at breakfast about Elliot Neil taking four cards and he feels better, his mind shifting again, across eyes, from his ma's to Audrey's, and then to Chelsea's, where it rests.

Elliot Neil tucks his lone card into the fresh four, and begins the long sort. "Still and all," Elliot Neil says, "it will be a great day."

Delancy leans back in his chair and chuckles. "Ah, it will, Elliot. Here's to it."

The men raise their glasses, the Jameson looking a little familiar to Albert, but still he brings it to his lips.

"Here's to marriage, and to children, and to a communion with God." Delancy's eyes are on him. He looks to the whiskey in his glass.

"Here, here," Father King says.

Slainte, and the men drink. Albert sets the whiskey quickly down. Delancy throws his cards to the tabletop. "Ah, shit. Watcha dealing me, Albert?"

"Nothing better than my own, I'm afraid." Albert

replaces his cards with a salmon round.

Topper says, "I'm going to pee."

"Does that mean you're out?" Elliot Neil asks.

Topper tosses his cards across Albert's, rises unsteadily from his chair. "If I'm not back in ten minutes, send for the paramedics." He heads through the door to the dining room.

Elliot Neil considers his cards.

And considers them.

And—

Delancy slams down his whiskey glass. "Oh, for Christ's sake! Every Saturday afternoon for forty-six years. That's two thousand Saturdays! If you added up all the minutes, ahk! I'd be a younger man. It's your fault we're old, Neil."

"You're old, Jimmy. I'm antiqued."

They are waiting for Topper O'Brien.

"The fucking prostate," Delancy says. Albert's watching Delancy's cigar smoke rise up into the fan and disappear. He might like a fan like that over his bed at home, though he wouldn't know where to buy one, and there was the Montessori, and they could probably use a new TV first, though his ma would never say so.

"Albert," Delancy says like it's what they've been talking about all along, "when are you going to make right by Eileen?"

When he'd seen Chelsea on the steps, it had been a revelation. Not like the tears off the statue of Mary that the sisters had wanted him to see as a boy, Albert watching the statue for an entire afternoon and seeing nothing, Sandy saying that he'd seen them, Albert not knowing to this day if his brother had or hadn't, but a revelation nevertheless. And now he would be with her and if things worked out, if things worked out between them, then everything would now be OK.

Blinking hard, drawing his eyes down the column of smoke to its source.

And Father King frowning, "Now, Jimmy."

Delancy rests a hand on King's forearm. "No harm meant. But as the best friend of his father, God guard him—"

Elliot Neil crosses himself, "God guard him."

"—I feel I have to raise this question every six months or so."

Albert brushes crumbs from the table into his hand, shaking them onto his plate, keeping his eyes down. "We're not sure yet."

"But you've got to set a date, Albert."

"Give it a rest, Jimmy," says Father King.

"I won't." Delancy sits up straighter. "It's Audrey's third birthday coming up, her third. And you cannot raise a daughter outside of God."

Albert restraightens the deck of cards, pulls at a loose thread around his left cuff.

"It's not right, Albert, and it's not proper, and your

67

father, God rest his soul in Heaven, can get no peace."

Staring into his shirtsleeve.

Delancy slaps the table, whiskey jumping from Albert's glass to his hand. "And neither can your poor mother, who loves you, Albert Fitzmorris, more than she loves Jesus Christ himself."

Father King's voice is firm, "Enough Jimmy. I mean it."

Delancy turns to the Father, stares at him for a moment, then sucks the last drops of whiskey from his glass.

"I'll make it right," Albert finally saying, and he's looking down at the carpet, wiping his hand against his sleeve, wishing a timer would go off in this room, to say that his time was up.

The clock above Delancy's head, the spin of the fan, the bang of the pots from the kitchen.

ALBERT, DORI, SANDY, Sandy's pregnant wife Colleen, Jimmy Delancy, Topper O'Brien and Elliot Neil. St. Sebastian's Mass. Up on the altar, Father King, finishing his Sunday sermon, an arm on either side of the pulpit's lectern, leaning in toward his notes.

"Life, then, is like a corned-beef dinner." Father King clears his voice, looks out across the parish. "With care and seasoning, comes tenderness. With haste and indiscretion, comes the sinewy gristle of neglect." Father King checks his notes a final time, nods, coughs, and smiles with a modest satisfaction.

Out the pot comes a big corned beef. Albert leaning over it, the steam up into his face, thinking he might have added another onion to the broth. The corned beef for Topper; next Sunday, baked oysters with shrimp creole. Colleen beside him, stirring the thump — *colcannon*, potatoes and kale, though you could make it with cabbage— her pregnant belly pressing against the heat of the stove.

The Fitzmorris house is Sunday busy: his ma organizing the table as she has every Sunday for fifty years; Father King filling the water glasses, wiping spots with his sleeve; Delancy bringing chairs, cackling about something with Topper O'Brien who's pouring a little whiskey for Elliot Neil. Something about Elliot and Topper's wives being missing this Sunday and how the three old men might go out later and score.

In the kitchen with Colleen and the Sisters, Cady and Margaret, lifting out the corned beef, ladling great potfuls of steaming cabbage, maque choux, carrots and the thump.

"How's it coming, Colleen?" Delancy asks. "I've been ready for this meal since last Sunday."

Albert carries the steaming platter to the table.

Topper claps his hands. "Hurrah!"

The table fills up with potatoes and cabbage and carrots and thump and okra for Elliot Neil and pots of dirty rice.

"It smells fine, Colleen, fine," says Father King, extinguishing a Pall Mall in the ashtray that's always set in front of his chair.

"She can cook, Sandy," Delancy says. Delancy motions at Colleen's pregnant belly with his cigar, "You ought to marry the girl."

Sister Margaret whacks Delancy with a napkin.

Sandy laughing, the big mustache powdered from a beignet he'd snatched on the ride out from the firehouse, helping Colleen down into her chair.

Albert beside his ma at the head of the table, wiping his hands on his apron, with Sandy on his left and Colleen, hoping they'd eat before the food got cold.

Sandy jiggles Albert's apron string, pink because his usual apron was in the hamper. "You're not going fruity on me, are you baby brother?" Sandy reaches out and pinches the inside of Albert's knee. Albert slaps his hand.

When the last glass is filled, Father King stands, coughs, raises his glass of red wine, coughs again, this sets him going—the Father reaching out for the table until finally he has to take a big sip of the wine to clear his throat. He raises his glass again. "To Jimmy Delancy, who six days from now will bring a new son into his family, through the sanctity of marriage. And to Dori Fitzmorris, for our beautifully restored robes. And to all the women, for this beautiful Sunday feast."

"Here, here," says Topper O'Brien.

Albert unties his apron, draping the back of his chair.

"And finally," Father King says, "as always, to our Brendan, may God rest his soul."

His ma shakes a little. Delancy briefly covers her hand with his own. May God rest his soul.

Amens and silence.

And then Delancy from his seat at the head of the table dramatically reaches for the big plate of meat. "Well, keep it from the sisters or there'll be nothing left."

Sister Cady sneers, Delancy draws back as if she might strike him, Sister Margaret grinning, revealing a missing front tooth. And the room is alive once more.

Then—with talk of Father King's homily, and the difficulty of making good thump, and how good the thump was, and who'd never had it, and how did Colleen make it, and it being revealed that Albert had, and Albert turning red, then making big stirring movements with his hands to show how much strength you need to put behind the mixing of thump—comes a knock at the Fitzmorris front door.

Sandy says, "I'll get it," kisses Colleen who's chatting down the table to his ma, Albert serving Topper, who's telling him about horses.

"Three aces, I had!" says Elliot Neil.

"You always were a shark," Sister Margaret laughs, as Delancy pours Sister Cady more whiskey.

"No, no more whiskey," Sister Cady protests. "Well, maybe just a drop."

Sister Margaret looking over, "Sister!"

Everyone laughs.

And standing on the porch are Audrey and Eileen.

"Jesus, Eileen. Where's Albert been hiding you?"

Eileen uncertain, her face not joyous like Sandy's. "No, I—he's supposed to see Audrey today."

Sandy throws open the screen door. "Hey, Al, it's Audrey and Eileen."

A hand on either side of his plate, motionless.

His ma standing, "Eileen—come in dear heart." She meets Eileen at the line between the front room and the kitchen, taking her by the arm, leading her in toward the table. "I'm so happy you could finally make a Sunday."

Audrey stays close to Eileen, one step behind her. "And you! Where have you been hiding all these days?"

Audrey meeting her eyes for a second, smiling. "I have a birthday soon."

"I know you have, my honey," his ma says, and she wraps Audrey in her arms, in a way that makes him stand, Audrey disappearing into his mother's yellow dress.

Standing. "Hi."

Eileen looks straight at him. "I can't stay."

Delancy turns in his chair. Her eyes stay on his eyes. Audrey and his ma.

72

"That's right," he says, quickly, nodding, at Delancy, back at Eileen, over at his ma, "She still has to work. You know, every Sunday."

Eileen's confusion scares him. She shakes her head, turns to his mother. "Albert's supposed to watch Audrey, because Hank—"

"—I thought that was next Sunday," he realizes he's shouted. He coughs a little, smiles at the eyes that are all now upon him.

Delancy stands and kisses Eileen on the cheek. "Sit down, Eileen. Christ all mighty—sorry Father—"

Father King nods.

"—we'd started to think you didn't like us."

Eileen hesitating, "Really, I just—"

"Nonsense. You sit right here." Delancy pulls out his chair.

He tries to control his voice, but now it seems too soft, "She really has to—"

"Sit." Delancy pushes Eileen into the chair, his ma hurrying an extra in from the front room. Delancy squeezes in, whispering something to his ma.

He will leave the table. If he leaves the table, Eileen will have to follow. To talk in private. On the front porch. Or in his room.

Delancy takes a big bite and begins. "Well, we were just talking about my Kara's wedding." Delancy smiles as he says this, winks at Topper who glances at Elliot Neil.

His eyes on Eileen, thinking.

73

"It's going to be a proud day, Jimmy," Elliot Neil says, his face inches from his big mound of okra. "Hi, Eileen."

"Hi, Mr. Neil. Hello, Father."

Audrey climbs into his ma's lap. She begins to tap on her belt buckle with a spoon.

"Nice to see you, Eileen," Father King says.

Sandy says, "Yeah. Hey, Al, maybe you and Eileen can double up with Colleen and me at the wedding. Al?" The tapping of the spoon, and his ma whispering to her, and she's singing Audrey a song, *she is handsome, she is pretty, she is the queen of Belfast city,* and Eileen's eyes on him, and Delancy's on her, and Elliot Neil talking, the tap on the buckle, the spin of the bar fans and the whirl of the carousel, the click of clocks above beds, the pills he'd give his da, the drip of fluid, the passing of days.

A pitch in his belly, he reaches for water, and he does not know what to do with her, there, in the face of all this, tapping along with his ma's singing, the whole room feeling separate and those in it, and he wants to holler out the blackness but instead swallows it in deeply, pressing it down and also tears. His hand goes out and quiets her spoon.

Audrey looks up suddenly, her round cheeks and the freckles. "Hank has a belt with a horsey on it."

He feels himself rising again, his hand across his daughter and his ma, floating upward. "Well, maybe you can stay over with little Hank sometime. If it's OK with Hank's mother."

Eileen looks up fast, "Albert!"

Standing now, he brings the hand into his hair. "I think Mommy has to work next Sunday. So I don't think we can join you, Sandy."

"For the wedding," Delancy says, "she ought to be able. Where are you working these days, Eileen? I'll talk to your boss."

He turns fast to Delancy. "Jimmy—

"Yes, Albert?"

Eileen stands, bumping the table, red wine slopping from her glass. "We have to go."

"Oh, no," his ma says.

"I'm . . . sorry," Eileen says, "I—come on, Audrey."

Audrey's got the spoon behind the drape of the table cloth, running it up and down, watching the ripple. "I want to stay with Dori."

Eileen speaks too quickly, "I said come on."

Sister Cady's eyes fall on her.

"Goodbye, dearheart," his ma says, "We'll see you soon." Kisses her forehead and her hands.

"Bye, Daddy."

Eileen grabs her hand. "Nice to see everyone. I'm . . . sorry." Hurrying to the front door, she doesn't look at him, pushing Audrey out, cross rocking at the screen door slap, cotton tuft falling to the floor.

And all eyes stare after her, confused; except Delancy's, whose face is turned to Albert.

And then Sister Cady coughs, cutting back into her

beef. Sister Margaret and Father King quickly do the same.

THE NEON CLOVER outside Delancy's Chop House glows off the windshields of the cars that are beginning to fill the parking lot of Jimmy Delancy's busy restaurant. Albert like a gunshot through the front door, past Maura the hostess, straight back and into the kitchen where Delancy is arguing with the chef.

"Goddamnit, Peter, I keep getting complaints," Delancy's saying, "This cannot go on."

"And *I* tell you that diners under two thousand years old have come to expect a little more creativity than a goddamned parsley garnish."

Albert slows.

"Oh, now, Peter, that's not fair," Delancy says. "I've always given my chefs plenty of latitude in the kitchen." Delancy looks over. "Hello, Albert."

Albert starts. "Jimmy, I—"

"But you're burning people's mouths with your gumbo. They don't like it, Peter, I'm telling you they don't like it."

The chef stiffens. "Well, I do—"

"Jimmy, I—"

"Listen, Peter, I want you to be creative, but I want you—"

"To do it your way."

"It's the customers."

"Jimmy," Albert says, "I've got to talk with you."

Jimmy Delancy turns, hard. "What is it, Albert?"

"Not in front of him."

"Good." The chef storms back to the ovens.

"Oh, Jesus." Delancy swings his arms down in disgust. "Albert, what?"

"Don't you ever talk to Eileen as you did today."

Delancy's eyes widen. "As I talked to her today?"

Backing down a little, "Just stay out of my affairs."

"Out of your—Jesus Christ, Albert, I can't see much of an affair to stay out of."

"I only mean . . . "

"Now you listen to me, you ungrateful, childish imp—" Delancy's body shakes. "Your own daughter doesn't kiss you hello or goodbye, your fiancee won't stay for dinner, never comes for Mass."

The veins in Delancy's neck swell.

"You're not a man, Albert Fitzmorris . . . if your father were here—"

"My father has nothing to do with this."

And Delancy's hand like a flash, and it slaps him, Albert seeing blackness, and a boat, and his father and Delancy pitching horseshoes in the backyard, his father shirtless, Delancy rushing the porch steps to help his mother with a tray of lemonade.

77

And then, suddenly, when the blackness clears, Delancy looking very old.

"Your father has everything to do with this."

Delancy past him, brown shoes squeaking across wet tile, Albert with a hand still to his cheek, Delancy unsteadily touching the green wood that frames his office door.

GREY GULLS CRUISE low along the Mississippi, at dawn, looking for surface fish, or more likely fish heads dumped illegally, the clean-up of Lake Pontchartrain narrowing their range. Grey sky, brown-black water.

Albert on a docked trawler, in his hip waders, keeping big fish from rolling off the belt. Watching the fish rise from the hold. Saying nothing. Terry at the dock with the bins.

"Hey, Al?"

Turns to Terry. "Yeah?"

"Fuck you."

Terry grinning.

"Hey, Al?"

Looking over again, Terry with his face pressed flat against a tuna's. He makes a kissing noise.

Albert nods, smiles a little, steps to the dock edge, Terry extending a hand.

"So what is it, Al? Your dream girl dump you already?"

Albert frowns. "I'm going out with her tonight."

Terry stepping back, eyes wide with exaggerated wonder. "Tonight! Shit, Albert, you're going to have to take off those waders."

Albert smiles. "Thanks."

He pulls off his gloves. Fish eyes stare darkly back at him from the bins, unblinking. He thinks of what Delancy said at the poker game, how his ma loved him more than she loved Jesus Christ himself. He knew his mother loved him and Sandy. She'd do just about anything for you. With his da's death, she did not need a further disappointment.

A smelt smacks his neck.

"Hey!"

A snapper slaps his jaw.

"You!"

Albert hoists a big fish, twirls, socks Terry with it in the ribs.

Terry laughing. Albert laughing.

The dockman down the boats turns from a conversation, yelling to the men he's known since they were boys. "Hey now! Pay for it first, you bastards."

Then Terry drops a fish tail down the front of Albert's waders and they erupt, Albert chasing Terry down the docks as the sun rises up over the mouth of the river.

• • •

ALBERT SITS ALONE on the streetcar, having seen the sun rising, now watching it set. In his blue windbreaker, his da's hat, clutching a record album that's wrapped in a brown paper bag.

Two schoolgirls, St. Sebastian's kids, in plaid skirts and navy sweaters, sniffing the air dramatically, rolling their eyes, giggling at Albert's fishy smell.

He removes the LP sleeve again from the bag. Holds the sleeve by its edges, careful not to smear it with his fingers. *Johnny Niles, The Thing is Love*—two lovers, holding each other close on a rainy city street, oblivious to the rush for shelter around them.

Above, to his left, on the streetcar's high tin ceiling, the pink steps of the Pinnacle Hotel: *Step into Luxury*. He slides the LP sleeve carefully back into the bag, holding the record just tight enough so it will be secure, up against his chest.

SHOWER WHOOSH and whistling, his hat on his windbreaker on a hook beneath the cross that hangs beside the door. Johnny Niles with "Fly Me to the Moon," the LP spinning on the old hi-fi. Horns kick in and Albert scrubbing himself in the shower stall, his body entirely covered with soap. Scrubbing and scrubbing with a thick hairbrush, his skin from pink to red.

Lathering, then shaving with a straight razor, from a porcelain shaving cup that once was his da's.

Whistling.

Towels off the final spots, douses, splashes Old Spice— on his cheeks, on his neck, through his chest hair, beneath his arms. Talcs, the wet hair grabbing the powder until he looks snowed.

He frowns at the reflection of his belly. He sucks his belly in. Lets it fall. Niles into a piano duet with a muted trumpet, egging, teasing, Albert getting into the spirit, sucking the big belly in, then out, to the beat; begins to simultaneously raise and lower his bushy eyebrows: in— out, up—down, in—out, up—down, as his ma arrives in the doorway.

She pauses.

"Ah, she's a lucky girl, lad."

Albert grins.

LOOKING IN THE window of Cora's Collecting, Chelsea at a set of vintage sterling cuff links, Albert at the reflection of him and her, him in his blue suit, Chelsea in a black dress, her slender arms, the lightness of her legs. He's happy he took her this way, past the back of the Cathedral where there was a garden, down along the narrow stone streets his father used to take him, his father telling stories about piracy, embarrassing Albert by pinching him when they walked past the homosexuals.

"I hope you don't mind us walking and all, but I've never had much use for a car."

She's holding the white rose he'd got her. She'd left it by mistake on the sill of the window at Cora's, but luckily he'd seen it.

"It's fine, Albert," she says.

At the pink steps of the Pinnacle Hotel, he turns to her. Grinning. "Well. Here we are. Step into luxury."

Chelsea smiles, but not as fully as he had imagined.

"I hope you haven't been here."

"No. No, I never have." She twirls the rose a little in her hands.

He takes her by the arm, lightly, thinking of the couple in the streetcar's tin ad as they ascend.

A quartet plays classical music in the corner of the Pinnacle Room, back behind the blonde wood bar, where the pink-swirled walls and the pink-swirled carpet meet. A hostess, in a dress like Chelsea's but blue, escorts Albert and Chelsea to a table against the restaurant's long window that overlooks the Quarter.

"And we have a wonderful special tonight." The hostess pulls out Chelsea's chair. "Fresh grouper."

Chelsea sits.

Albert sits, glancing around, nodding approvingly. The

dining room's as nice as the one at the Blue Royale Hotel, maybe nicer.

Chelsea's got the white rose in her hands. "Could you bring me a vase for this?"

"Sure." Chelsea's eyes follow the hostess, and he wants them back. He's grinning, slightly, he cannot help it.

Think of something to say.

He clears his throat. "It's, um, nice that you could stay at the table for a change."

Chelsea laughs, "Yeah, Albert, it is."

Nodding. "I was going to get you a dozen flowers, you know, but I wasn't sure how you'd carry them."

"It's a nice thought, Albert." She smiles.

Feeling his ears go hot, he drinks from his glass of water. "It never did storm," he says. And then her eyes meet his and he keeps drinking, until the entire glass is drained.

A waiter arrives behind Albert, announces himself, "Good evening." Ice slides from the glass to his cheek to the table. "Can I bring you wine?" the waiter asks.

"Of course." Blotting the spill with his cuff.

"Very good."

"Yes."

The waiter is smiling.

"Oh, well, yes. Let my date choose it." Nodding at Chelsea. "Whatever you want, Chelsea. I'll drink anything." Closing his eyes at his remark.

"Do you have a Rivard Manor, chardonnay?"

The waiter bows slightly and is gone.

Chelsea rests her bare forearms on the table, her hands at her chin like she's praying. "So, you live here, in New Orleans?"

"Sure. My whole life."

"You just like hotel dining rooms?"

"Oh, sure."

He's grinning and he's trying to stop doing so. Chelsea sips her water. He watches her lips, taking the water like a delicate bird. Watches her hand as it lowers the glass, rises back up to her chin.

"You must travel a lot with your business."

On the table are the rolls and butter and he can't help noticing that, either.

"Yeah," he says, "every morning on the streetcar downtown, every afternoon on the streetcar uptown."

Albert laughs. Chelsea does, too.

"You live uptown. That's nice."

She picks up a roll, places it on her plate. He butters one and bites into it. "How about you? You live uptown?"

"No, I'm afraid I could never afford it on a restaurant salary. Not in your neighborhood, anyway." He stops chewing, as he takes this in.

The hostess brings a bud vase and the wine. She's staring at Chelsea. "Don't I know you? I mean, not to be rude."

"I'm your twin at the Blue Royale."

"Yeah? I applied for a job there. You like it OK?"

He tries to fit the rose into the slender vase. The stem's too wide with the thorns. He glances at Chelsea who's not watching, then shoves it in.

Smiles.

"Sure," Chelsea says.

The hostess pops the wine, sets the cork in front of him. He picks it up, holds it to the light, looks at it a little bit, then brings it to his nose, and sniffs it. "Fine."

The hostess pours him a sample. He sips it. "Fine." Then, just in case, he sniffs it, too. "Fine."

The hostess smiles. He's feeling like he's got a rose-thorn in his thumb. "I'm Elizabeth, if you need me."

He does have a thorn in his thumb. He picks it out fast, reaches down, casually, and blots his thumb with his sock.

"Well, cheers," Chelsea says.

His necktie's on the dinnerplate.

"Cheers."

Albert folds his necktie smoothly back across his chest. Their glasses touch.

"Delicious," Chelsea says.

That dew again, gently across the top of her lips. He sips a little more fully from his glass.

A streetcar clatters in the distance, its lights trace the Quarter. He watches her watch it, her face seeming suddenly sad.

"Yes," he says, and he breathes in, his chest filling. Breathes out. "Do you like your job?"

She turns from the disappearing train. She rolls her

eyes. "Oh, God, don't bring up work."

"Oh, no, I didn't mean to imply nothing—anything—you know, ha, ha, I don't even like my job." Looks out the window himself.

"What do you do?" she asks.

Two teenagers neck beneath a yellow light in the alcove of a jeweler.

"Fish."

"Fish?"

Trying to muster courage. "I'm in the seafood business." Turns from the window. Stares into the rose. It is a first date. He wouldn't mind talking about his job at Bobby's, but he does not feel like getting into it now. To make an impression. And he'd rather hear about her.

Chelsea bites into her roll. "Oh, well, this is certainly the place for it. I know a man in breading, just breading, that's all he sells. He's got a house on Grand Isle and another in France."

Albert laughs, nervously. He quickly fills both their glasses, though his is barely touched.

"How about you?" he asks. "*Do* you like your job?"

"You really want to know?"

"Yeah."

Watching the gold now that waves around her neck as she sips, thinking about the beauty that lies above it and below.

"It's like this, Albert." He brings his eyes to hers.

"You're a girl who was never much good in school, who people paid attention to because she has blonde hair and ... whatever. I can't type, I don't want to work in an office. I modeled for a while, locally, but then you get too old."

She drops her eyes from him.

"Albert, there's not a lot for a girl like me to do."

Gazing at the music and candlelight of her eyes.

"Sure there is, Chelsea; there's lots a girl like you can do."

She smiles.

"That's sweet of you, Albert. You know that's why I agreed to go out with you. When you picked up that old woman's glasses. A lot of guys, well, they aren't sweet."

"Like that guy who drove the Jaguar?"

Her smile fades. "How do you know about Robert?"

"I'm sorry, I didn't mean—I saw the two of you there, when you were working." She doesn't seem angry; she's eyeing the pink edges of the rose.

"Oh, yeah, well, yes, like that man in the Jaguar."

She looks at her wine glass, then up at him.

"That's the other thing, Albert. There's not many men for a girl like me, not many good ones anyway."

She lifts the glass. "I mean they just want to take you to bed. That's all they want, Albert, a good . . . whatever."

He brings his glass quickly to his lips, trying not to look away.

"And then—" she shakes her head "—then they turn out to be something they said they weren't."

She drinks fast, in two long swallows. Seeing this, he does the same. Then he quickly fills her glass, and his own.

Chelsea hangs on Albert's arm. Beneath the moss that drapes down from balconies, under the colored lights, Chelsea's drunk, she's laughing, speaking softly into Albert's neck, two inches taller than he. He feels her breath.

She's saying, "But that's how she is Albert: gone, completely gone. Loopy. I told her, 'at the fourth husband I draw the line.' I mean I'll send her a gift, but I'm not flying to Jacksonville. Even if she is my mother. Oh!" Beneath a cloud of begonias. "Here's where I live!"

The front steps damp, water dripping from a cracked gutter pipe that runs the length of the shuttered Quarter house, begonias flowing from the balcony above.

"It's nice," Albert says.

Chelsea's digging in her purse. "Oh, it is. I had to get it from someone who knew someone who knew someone." Her keys hang from a gold letter C. One foot on her frontstep, the other on the sidewalk, his hands folded at his waist. She is smiling, swaying slightly. She steps toward him. "That's my balcony, Albert. Maybe one day you can serenade me."

She wraps an arm around his neck from the side, pointing to the balcony overhead. He swallows, thickly.

"Sure. I'll be your Cyrano."

"You want to come up, Cyrano?"

When he looks down his cheek presses against the warmth of her arm. It warms through him.

He hears, "I mean, you know, I could use a cup of coffee," as her arm slips away.

"I knew what you meant."

He cannot meet her eyes.

Chelsea puts both hands on her door key and guides it into the lock. "That's one thing I like about you, Albert. You know, how you live with your mother, how you take care of her. So many people, in your position, they'd just send her away, to Palm Beach or something. It's very sweet."

Turns his face toward hers, but she's already in the building, holding open the door.

"It's not much," she says.

"It's nice."

The ceiling is high, nearly as high as the studio is long. An iron bed in one corner, bedcovers everywhere; a small white kitchen, Albert thinking it'd be cramped to prepare a meal for more than one or two; a café table with two chairs; a loveseat in front of a TV, with a fireplace and the French windows that he's looking out, the room behind him reflected, the city spread down the end of the street below.

"Well," Chelsea says from the kitchen, "the fireplace is nice. And the windows."

"Yeah."

She moves to the French doors, unsteadily, and opens them. The river breeze blows her hair, catching and scattering the light from the street.

Her shoulders and the slope down the back of her dress.

Frozen in the middle of her room.

"Come see."

She trips a bit on the lip between the inside and the out. Into the night air and the ship horns of riverboats, the hush of traffic, and the laughter from the city streets below.

She leans on the iron railing of her balcony, staring down the alleyway to the swirl of the lights beyond. Albert stands two steps behind her, the distance between them feeling like hell's fire.

"We were supposed to go to the Caribbean. Montserrat," she says, not looking at him. Streetlights golden across her skin, the moon up above. He steps beside her, staring straight ahead, at the empty balcony across the narrow alley.

"We were supposed to . . . just get away."

She turns her face to his and there are tears in her eyes and, with a breath, before he fully realizes that he has done it, he covers her hand with his own. Just leaves it there, the warmth rising up his arm and into his head.

Turning, slightly, to see her face. Her eyelids start to close. She moves toward him and then her eyes open and she blinks them. "Woo, Albert, I better fix that coffee."

He quickly pulls away his hand, nodding.

She touches his shoulder. She stumbles at the doorway's lip, steadies herself in the door frame, and goes inside.

Alone, in the middle of the flower-edged balcony, all around him the moon and the breeze and the heat from the street, the thick smell of flowers, the night clouds drifting to the beating of his heart.

Stepping inside, he can't help but see Chelsea, in her bathroom, her dress around her ankles, a black bra tight across her skin.

"Ah, Jesus."

He quickly looks away. Looks again: she's pulling a jersey across the curves of her back. In the bathroom doorway, pale, in just the jersey, hair tumbling across her face.

"I'll make you that coffee, now, Albert," she says. Her words slurring. "I just need to lie down."

Chelsea steps toward her bed, makes it halfway, then folds down to the carpet, her head to the edge of her mattress.

He rushes to her. "Chelsea!"

Wraps her in his arms, to bring her to bed. Her face

buries into his neck. Her breasts press toward him as he lifts.

He sets a knee on her mattress so as to lower her. What with the wine he himself has had, his balance topples, and he tumbles to the mattress beside her.

For a moment, he does not move.

Above them, her ceiling fan spins.

His head is pinioned, such that no matter how far to the right or left he glances, he can see only the gold of her hair. Shifting, craning his head gently, quietly up to see.

She's spread beside him, her bare arm across his chest, her jersey bunched so that the black of her underwear shows.

"Albert—"

Albert whipping his head back to the fan. She curls her body against his, pressing her cheek to the blue lapel of his suit, feeling her heart beat and feeling his own. Hers slow. His like a piston. He was drunker than this when Audrey was conceived; he's glad that he's soberer now.

The river breeze winds in. Through her chimes, across a paper wind lantern that twirls unlit at her bedside.

Lightly, gingerly, resting his right arm about her small waist, holding her. Her breath feeling warm against the cloth against his chest.

Whispering. "You know, Chelsea, I always wanted to get away, too, to do something anyway. My brother, Sandy, he got away, joined the Coast Guard. Now he's a fireman." He extends his neck again, his breath at the edge of her hair. "But when my father died, I don't know. I guess I just never made it. Not yet anyway."

He smiles a little. Chelsea does not stir. He lets his lips linger, feeling her heat, breathing deeply her soft scent. "Chelsea?" She is sleeping. He lifts her from him, sliding his arm from beneath her. He lowers her head carefully to the pillows and stands.

He gathers the bedsheets, smoothes them, and lays them across her. Her foot sticks out. He takes it in his hands. Holding it, softly, runs his thumb lightly along the sole, and then he tucks it in.

He deadbolts the balcony's doors, shuts off the kitchen and bathroom lights. At the doorway of her studio, he turns, his face in the moonlight that catches off the fan.

"Good night, Chelsea," he whispers, and he lets his eyes linger. She's curled now in the bedsheet and blanket, warmth all through his blood. "Sweet dreams to you." And he steps quietly into the hallway, gently closing her apartment door.

3

A newspaper boy rides his bicycle down the misted street, avoiding the pot holes and rusted out car parts, chased by a dog, the boy whistling to himself as he rides.

Inside the Fitzmorris home, his ma's got a coffee cup suspended halfway between her cornflakes and her lips, across the kitchen from Albert, who's in his good blue slacks, a clean white shirt, and's whistling along with Johnny Niles' cover of "Tea for Two."

Glides over to his ma, sliding fresh-cut strawberries onto her cereal from a bowl.

"This is getting worse and worse! What next, dancing girls?"

He flips the spoon into the air, catches it.

"Since when is Eileen such a drinker? Since when are you such a whistler? And further more—" Albert flips the spoon again. "Stop that, come back here."

He stands before his ma. She presses a hand to his forehead. "No fever."

She pokes him in the gut. "No loss of appetite."

"Hey cut that out, you old woman."

"And what's with the fancy clothes? Bobby Kelly finally going respectable?"

"I'm tired of looking like a slob."

She brushes a toast crumb from his shirt. "Well, I must say, for a drunkard you look pretty good." She straightens his too-short necktie. "But from a slob to Sinatra?"

She takes her bowl across to the sink and rinses it.

"I haven't heard 'Tea for Two' since I was a girl. And I didn't like it then!"

She reaches for the row of pills that she swallows each morning. "Listen, Albert, why wouldn't Eileen stay for the Sunday meal?"

Albert's left the kitchen.

"Albert!"

He emerges from his bedroom, sporting a brand new tweed cap.

"Oh, now this is too much."

She grins, meets her son at the table.

"Listen, dearheart. Your old mother's busy enough now with the *Delancy* wedding."

He makes a fish face at her.

"Stop that." Her old eyes alive and happy. "At least give us a little notice, lad, before you set the date."

He grabs his hat.

She's into the front room closet, pulling on her coat.

"You teaching today, Ma?"

"I'm going out to Versailles with Father King and two nuns from the Sisters of Mercy. King wants to do some sort of exchange. It'll be cute, all those Vietnamese kids."

"Versailles? Who's driving?"

"One of the sister's brothers has a Lexus." She slips her eyeglasses case into the coat pocket. "I told King we'd cruise the convent afterwards."

He holds the front door open. There's no stopping her, even as she has trouble getting down their front steps, even as there's a chill in the air that he worries will catch up to her. But it's good that she's busy. When his da died, she didn't leave the house for three months, and then suddenly she was busier than ever. She taught, she worked the gardens at the hospital, and last fall she took his father's place as campaign manager for Topper's re-election as president of the Irish Channel St. Patrick's Day Club, even as Topper had lived in Broadmoor since before Albert was born.

"Maybe I'll call her."

"You got your keys, Ma?"

He's locking their door behind him. They've got a sticker that says "Armed Patrol" above the door handle that Terry stuck there, but all they had was a TV and a broken VCR and the stereo and if any burglers wanted, say, the old stove they could have it. He knows better than to walk her down the steps, so he walks beside her, as if by chance.

"I realized Sunday just how long it's been since I've seen her," she continues.

At the foot of their steps he turns to her.

"Ma?"

"Eileen, Albert." She's unfolding a plastic rain hat,

spreading it across her hair, tying it under her chin. "You're familiar with her."

A bottle's been smashed on the sidewalk and he bends down to clean it up. "Well, she's busy, Ma," but he can tell he's speaking too softly, as if he's nearly lost his voice.

"Albert. I know she's busy. That's why we'll make plans."

The glass jumping around in his hand. He loosely closes his fist. "I'll have her call you, Ma."

He nods, stands, and turns toward the barrels. "She's got a new phone and all." He steps into the alley between the houses.

He closes his eyes. She'll know he has the number. He lifts the barrel lid. Inside, on top, there's a Schwegmann's bag full of green fragment scraps, and a box of wavey cardboard stars whose edges must have been cut when his ma's hand was not steady.

A car horn sounds.

The glass in his hand. His ma at the curb, her blue rain scarf and blue coat. He closes the lid on the can.

The Lexus pulls up and it's black with a red spoiler and a license plate that reads "GoSnts." His ma gets in with Father King and the Sisters of Mercy, and the Sister who's driving makes a wide U-turn and beeps the horn again, his mother waving from the back seat, Father King tightly clutching the door frame, an unlit Pall Mall hanging from his lip.

. . .

Inside Bobby Kelly's, Terry slaps a giant sea bass on the cold steel counter.

"Oh, come on, Fitz," Terry says. "Did you nail her or didn't you?"

"She's not that kind of person."

Albert chops off the fish's head with two big cuts.

"Yeah? Where did you take her?"

He runs a bone-blade the length of the spine. "A place you wouldn't know about." Digs his fingers along the vertebrae and pulls the flesh from the bone. "The Pinnacle House."

"The Pinnacle House!" Terry sets his knife loudly to the counter. "Jesus, Fitz, you took her to a hotel dining room?"

Albert, uneasy. "Sure."

Terry tosses the fish head into the bin.

Albert watches the flies leap out, for a moment, blankly.

"Albert, she *works* in a hotel dining room." Terry shakes his head.

Albert peeling flesh from the bone. Fish juice squirts out, drawing a line down his clean undershirt.

"You got to take her somewhere classy, Fitz."

"She liked it."

Quickly puts a fresh towel beneath the tap, wipes at the juice.

"Take her on the riverboat."

"The riverboat?" He lifts the shirt to his nose. Smells OK.

"Oh yeah." Terry turns to his friend. "Prime rib, all you can eat. They've got a band—"

"She likes music."

"And after dinner, you take a little stroll along the deck—"

Terry blows him a couple of kisses. Albert frowns.

"Jesus, Al, you did at least kiss her?"

He turns his back, slaps the meat on the hanging scale. "I got her flowers."

Terry nodding, encouraged. "Yeah? That's good. Flowers are good."

Albert looks around, lowers his voice. "They're in the fridge. They're roses. I wrapped them in plastic so they wouldn't stink."

"Roses. Now you're talking, Al. Let me see the card."

"Terry—"

"Come on, Albert. You want to do this thing right, or what?"

He wraps his hand with another clean towel, reaches into his t-shirt pocket, and carefully removes a small paper card, the card-face printed with a steaming cup of coffee.

Terry reaches for it, but he makes him wrap his hand in a clean towel as well. Terry reads the card out loud, "Dear Chelsea—I would like to see you again soon. Maybe for that cup of coffee? Ha. Ha.—Albert Fitzmorris."

Terry just stares at the card.

"Ha, ha. Albert Fitzmorris . . . ?"

"Come on now Terry, lay off it."

"Why don't you invite her to fucking high tea or something?"

"It's an insider's joke."

"An insider's—"

Terry puts an arm across Albert's tensed shoulders. "We'll get a card at lunch."

AT THE RECEPTION desk of the Blue Royale Hotel, a wispy clerk has one hand on the roses, waiting for Albert to let go. Albert, in his white shirt, his short red tie, reminding the clerk of what he's already told him twice. "They're for Chelsea."

The clerk sighs, "I didn't suppose they were for me."

"You'll make sure she gets them?"

The clerk eyes the bouquet, the thin stems, the slightly frozen flowers. "Definitely."

Albert reluctantly releases his grip.

"Is there a card?"

"Of course."

He turns from the clerk slightly, unbuttons two shirt buttons, and reaches inside his dress shirt to the pocket of the fish-stained undershirt.

He checks the card: *Dear Chelsea—Please be my River*

Rose. Fondly, Albert. Terry, he thinks, was probably right about him not needing to write "Fitzmorris."

The clerk's hand is out. He hesitates, then places the card into the clerk's hand, along with two rumpled dollar bills.

Walks quickly back across the lobby.

IN A ROUGHER section of the Quarter, Saturday morning sun on his neck, Albert buzzing the two-story duplex, balancing a cake tin in his hands. Sun bouncing off the old stone building, off the red graffiti that someone's sprayed over the blue.

He buzzes some more. Shakes his head. Tries the beat-up knob of the steel-grate security door. The door's unlocked.

Climbing the wood steps, present in his pocket, the cake tin in his hands. His ma hadn't remembered to buy the blue food coloring, but he'd gotten lucky when the Food Quick had it, just before midnight, next to the women's personal hygiene products.

At the balloons, he knocks. No answer. Music, kids laughing. He pounds. That door's open too. He steps inside.

Eileen's flat's got kids everywhere, in hats and birthday clothes, screaming, chasing each other. Audrey, in chaps and a space hat, watching him.

"Hi, Daddy."

Picking her up, to bring her cheek to his. "Hi."

She blows a toy trumpet in his ear.

"Hank got me my trumpet," showing him, keeping the smile on his face.

He sets her down. "Where's your mother?"

"In the kitchen."

In the kitchen, Hank's doling out soda to a sea of outstretched arms. "All right, all right, hold on, who wants whiskey with their soda pop?"

Albert, beneath a happy birthday banner, unnoticed, watching. Hank, his gray beard, nearly a foot taller than him, a decade older, black. Eileen, the mother of his child, who had once let him hold her in his arms, with whom he'd once thought he'd find a closeness, a nearness, to love.

She'd met Hank at AA. He'd been married once, to a woman who also drank, who drank and took his own son. He was good to Audrey and no longer drank and the one time Albert had heard Hank play trumpet, the time when he thought he and Eileen were maybe on a date at Shipwreck's Supper Club, he'd liked the way Hank played. His playing was mournful, like he'd had a rough go of things. Later—after Eileen had told him that she and Hank were together—she'd told him about Hank's son, and he'd thought about that playing, and it had caused any hatred in him to go.

Eileen turns, Albert holding the cake tin out in front of him. She smiles. "Hey, Al—"

"The door was open . . . I brought a cake."

Eileen takes his arm, leads him from the doorway into the kitchen. "That's really sweet of you. Hank, Albert's brought a cake."

Hank looks up from his pouring. "That's great. How you been, Albert?"

Albert nods, half-smiles toward Hank. "Fine, you know, great."

Eileen's got a thumb under the cake tin rim. The cover pops off. He hopes it's all right. He had a little difficulty getting Madeline's eyes right; he had to consult the book he'd bought, but her coat came out well, he'd mixed a little green in with the blue, and mostly he thought it looked OK.

"It's beautiful."

He feels himself flush. He does not want to flush in front of her.

"It's really sweet of you, Albert."

He indicates the direction of the front door with his head. "Yeah, well, the front door was unlocked, Eileen."

He's not sure why he's said it.

"OK, everyone," Hank says. Hank leads the kids out, trailing soda from their too-full cups.

Eileen lifts the cake from the tin. "The door was unlocked, Albert, because we couldn't hear the buzzer."

"Well, the building door, too. Anyone could just walk in and—"

"Hank's here."

Eileen puts four candles on the cake, the fourth for luck.

The kitchen door swings back open. Audrey there, helmet off, grinning.

Hank lifts a giant, store-bought, half-eaten cake from the coffee table, puts it by a lamp in the living room's far corner. Eileen coming through the kitchen door, his Madeline cake lit with candles, leading the kids—tigers, Mardi Gras Indians, vampires—in "Happy Birthday."

Happy Birthday to You. Some kid makes a farting noise and the other kids laugh.

Eileen cuts into Madeline.

"I want a piece from the other cake," says a pirate.

Albert takes a big breath and steps into the room. Smiling, he sits on the carpet beside his daughter. She rests her hand on his leg. She's got a pink tattoo of a rocket on her forearm. She's got three plastic bracelets on her wrist and a big green ring on her finger that makes a winking eye.

He raises his eyebrows, digs into his windbreaker pocket, pulls out a small box, wrapped in gold, bound in lavender ribbon.

"I hope you like it," he says to her, smiling again. "I had to look all over for it, Audrey, for just the right one."

Eileen kneels beside him. He smiles at her, nodding toward the box that Audrey's rapidly unwrapping. Audrey pulls off the lavender ribbon, the gold paper, lifts the cover of the white box inside. The kids around him running and Hank across from him and Eileen, and he is sweating, looking down at the grey tissue that's held together with a golden seal, the seal scrolled with the name of the jeweler.

Eileen's face tightens. "Albert?"

And he feels suddenly, there with Audrey beside him and the kids and the balloons and Eileen, a feeling that he's mistaken, that he's about to do something wrong, and he's watching the beads of the bracelets, the yellow, the pink, the blue that slide up and down her wrist and the freckles and the winking eye as she tears at the paper. It is all he can do to keep himself from reaching out and stopping her. He stands.

Audrey breaks the seal and reaches into the tissue. She pulls out the flat, gold necklace; a necklace just like Chelsea's, but smaller, it had cost him his after-taxes salary for a week.

"Pretty," Audrey says.

She swings it around.

"It's a necklace," he's saying. "It's gold."

"Albert," Eileen says, and she is falling away from him, his eyes on the necklace, too big in his daughter's small hands. "What's the deal? What's going on?"

"You clasp it." His hands are shaking. He had not imagined it this way. When he made the cake he'd been thinking about the necklace, of her face when he gave it to her.

Freckles on the back of her neck. "Thanks, Daddy." Red hair and her eyes. She stands. Blows her toy trumpet. Marching. The chain low around her neck. Poking Hank in the belly with her horn, marching circles around Hank's legs.

"Albert," Eileen begins, softly.

"Excuse me."

Crossing fast, wrapping paper crunching beneath his shoes.

He hurries open the bathroom door. A kid in a cowboy outfit pushes past him, zipping up his fly. Behind them, laughter again, and now music.

Albert shuts the door and locks it. He turns both taps on loud. Cups his hands, fills them, douses his face with water. Again. A third time. All things in threes.

Looks at himself in the mirror, water trailing down his face like dumb tears.

A knock.

Ignores it.

A pound.

"Just a minute," he says.

He wipes his face with his sleeve, planning his route from the bathroom to the front door, so that he'll be able to at least tell her good-bye. He opens the bathroom door, hard. A ballerina's bouncing up and down.

He stands in the short hallway. In the living room, a couple of kids wrestle on the rug. Audrey and Hank are dancing.

He blinks a few times, watching, as Audrey twirls. He steps into the room across the hall.

Sheets in a bunch on the futon inside, a cluster of white candles like an altar at the bedside, crayon drawings filling the wall at the head of the bed. Stepping closer. Her drawings have been labeled in crayon by Eileen. He recognizes Eileen's handwriting. She'd sent him a note once, after she'd left. A short note, it talked about the AA third step and apologized to him for, as she'd put it, taking advantage of his good nature. He never answered that note. His father was dying and he gave his attention there.

A green splotch reads 'trees'; a blue one 'sky.' Further up the wall is a red scribble that's labeled 'fish.' He smiles at that one. In the middle of it all, a paint-by-number, of blue horses and a blue river, and for a moment he does not recognize it as the one from over Eileen's girlhood bed.

Fresh candles and used ones, the altar at St. Sebastian's, his da up above the fire and smoke, and on the bedside table two scribbled circles are framed. "Mommy" is one and the one with short hair and a beard reads "Hank."

LATER IN THE afternoon and he hears Delancy yell, "What the hell's he doing in there?" the old man's tough voice rolling down the corridor to the Chop House men's room where Albert's standing at the sink. "Albert, you're not old enough for those troubles."

Avoiding the sink, the water across his face reminding

him of Eileen's, and Audrey, dancing around with Hank. There's a window that pops out to let the air in, eye level, and he's looking out it, across the empty Chop House parking lot, out to the street, the street wavering with heat. Fast-food chicken restaurants, sagging telephone wires, a liquor store with bars on the windows.

"Albert!"

Out the far end of the lot, a Baptist church, a wedding streaming out, a black bride and her young groom, slim and handsome, and Albert seeing that couple on the Johnny Niles LP cover when they kiss.

Pulls open the men's room door, the wood paneled Chop House corridor dark and narrow. Wipes the sill's grit from his chin.

"Do you know," he can hear Elliot Neil saying, "that I can't fit into my tuxedo anymore? I had to have it taken in. The whole thing was like a sack."

"You're shrinking, that's why," Topper O'Brien says, loud, his hearing aid in need of an adjustment. "We all are. I went to kiss my grandniece the other night at dinner and I almost got her on the tit."

Just outside the side office, Delancy's hung a picture of himself as a boy with his own Irish father. Albert looks at the photo, a Depression-era, Irish Channel shotgun house, Delancy small and smiling, Delancy's father wiry and cold. In the space between the man and the boy you could fit another man.

"Shrinking my ass." Delancy's shaking his head as Albert comes through the door. "I'm the same size as in my fighting days. Albert—" Delancy yells, Albert stepping into the room.

"Here I am," Albert says. Half-smile, his eyes feeling red, hoping the men don't notice.

"Albert, if it's not asking too much, I'd like to get a couple hands in before I meet the Lord."

He takes his seat between Topper and Father King.

Staring into the center of the table. It was natural that she should like Hank. After all he had nothing against him, except that he left the doors open and maybe didn't make a salary that was steady.

"It's your deal, Albert," says Father King.

"Sorry." He picks up the cards and deals.

"And we're playing?" says Delancy impatiently, match burning in front of a White Owl.

"Five card," Albert says, "Sorry."

He could maybe take up an instrument as well. If she was going to be musical. He had played the trumpet for a year at St. Sebastian's after Sandy had graduated and it was assumed that Albert would fill Sandy's chair in the band. That hadn't worked out, but maybe he could try again.

"You don't look well, Albert," Father King says, his voice drifting in and Albert feeling suddenly tired.

"He looks well enough to deal. Some winners for a change."

Dealing the cards, his hands are wet and he wipes his right hand between his arm and his ribs and feels the dampness that coats his skin.

And the cards have bicycles on them and he sees Audrey on a bike, Hank pushing her, Eileen jumping up and down in the driveway.

"Jesus Christ," Albert hears himself say, and then the wave clears and Father King and Elliot Neil are looking at him.

"Sorry, Father," he says, and Father King nods, but still looks at him like something's not right.

He wipes his face with his shirtsleeve. He's never sick, but feeling like he has a fever. Shuts his eyes and presses his forearm for a moment hard against them. When he lowers his arm and opens his eyes, all the men are watching him. He smiles at them, weakly.

"The birthday party wore me out, I guess," he says, straightening the deck, restraightening until glancing up he sees the men have gone back to their cards.

Delancy makes a sucking noise with his lips, half-watching his hand, half-watching Albert. "Another birthday without a Godfather. Or any father for that matter." Delancy glances at his cards. "Of course, I've been told to butt out."

He deals Topper three, does not look at Delancy, and turns to Elliot Neil. Elliot Neil straightens slightly in his chair.

"Just the one card please, Albert," Neil says.

Delancy seems to choke. "What!"

"One card—" the cigarette seems to jump from Father King's lips.

"Elliot—" Delancy spits into his napkin, "—you haven't taken one card since the Eisenhower administration."

"A time for everything," Neil says.

Delancy settles with a long drink from his tumbler. "You should take Mr. Neil's attitude, Albert," Delancy says, smacking his lips. "A time for everything." Delancy chuckling. "That's Ecclesiastes, isn't it Father? For everything there is a season."

Father King's still staring at Elliot Neil. "Are you really only taking one card, Elliot?"

"That's right," Neil says.

"And you wouldn't bluff us, me, Elliot, after all these years, not counting that I'm a man of the Parish?"

Elliot Neil looks steadily at the Father. "Let's not push it, Richard."

He's trying to think of something good. Of sunlight, and when he first saw Chelsea, focusing on the heat of Chelsea's breath through his shirt on his chest but even that will not stay. Wondering if he might be sick, the cake and that goddamned gold chain and her dancing, wondering if he would pour blackness from his gullet and even from his pores.

• • •

Chips falling to the floor, whiskies slopping, ashes rising, opening his mouth, the thickness through his tongue, gasping, saying nothing, turning, and rushing out the door.

HE HADN'T BEEN sleeping much lately, the light from the street seeming brighter around the shade, his thoughts running to boats. His da on a boat, himself on a boat, the rope coiling around his leg, pulling him not into the Gulf but into the hold with the fish, where he'd look up to see Delancy closing him in. And Audrey on a paddleboat in City Park, them paddling together, her small legs working the pedals until they were working too fast, and Albert couldn't tell her to stop, was trying to but couldn't speak, and her just pedaling and pedaling, Albert waking with the sheet across his face, smothering him.

At four he'd been on the floor doing sit-ups. He'd started after his first date with Chelsea, with twenty-five, and now he was up to thirty. With push-ups he was stronger, squeezing out fifty with only a few breaks, touching his chest not just his belly to the floor.

At six his ma catches him in the kitchen flexing his right biceps in the window above the sink.

"Just coffee, Atlas," she says. "I'm off to market to help Jimmy Delancy with the flowers."

He wonders if Delancy would tell her about the game, about the way he'd left before it was finished.

"The wedding's not for a week," he says.

"Yes, but we have to order the flowers, and Jimmy wants me there, you know, to hold his hand."

He refills his coffee cup for the third time in the half hour, pours his ma's with hot milk from the stove.

She sips the coffee, the milk frothing her lip. "That's nice," she says.

He laughs, suddenly sees the down on Chelsea's cheek. "You got a mustache, Ma."

She dips her mouth deeper into the froth, looking up at him with a big milky lip. "That's not a nice thing to say to an old woman, Albert."

Laughing, but the way she laughs is different, like she's not entirely there. She's smiling, but it's the smile she's developed lately, his da's near the end if you asked him how he felt. His father always answered that he felt fine, fine—to Jimmy Delancy or Topper O'Brien he might add fine enough for your sister—but behind the smile was blackness. He wonders, again, what she knows.

"You take your pills, Ma?" He takes a pill from each of five bottles on the shelf above the sink.

"Albert, you bringing Eileen to the wedding?"

A pill falls to the basin.

He fishes with his fingers and he is unsteady and the pill slides into the drain. "I can't go alone."

The toast pops and he hurries a piece on her plate.

"Listen, Albert," she bites into the toast. "Friday, we've got the rehearsal dinner. You're my date. Jimmy wants us all there, you know, all Brendan's family."

"Sure, Ma."

"And in the morning I promised Father King that you'd help him with the chairs."

"Chairs?"

"You know, whatever. Just so he has some help. And Al, will you drop the robes off to the Father? He said he'd be in at lunchtime."

"Sure, Ma."

"It'll be a great day, Albert. Kara's a lovely girl."

She swallows the pills, the flesh on her neck loose and her hands not just dry but thinner than he'd recently noticed.

"Eat your toast," he tells her, and grabs a piece from the toaster himself. He's not ready to eat breakfast at the table, with the jitters from the coffee and the lack of sleep, despite the appetite the exercise has worked up.

His mother bites into the bread, whatever was on her mind seeming to have vanished. "You remember Sandy's Colleen? Ah, Albert, there's nothing more beautiful than a woman on her wedding day."

She bites into the toast again, and Albert feeling suddenly better, him with Chelsea on the steps of the Blue Royale Hotel, wearing a tuxedo that fits.

BESIDE THE CONFESSIONAL, the box of stitched robes in his arms, looking for Father King. He hadn't been inside the confessional since high school; Father King always inviting him, saying he could confess to another priest if he liked, that that's what Elliot Neil does. But Albert never having anything to say. Or, rather, having things to say, but not things he could say to Father King, his father's friend. But he couldn't say them to a stranger, either.

Feeling like maybe he can talk to Chelsea, who had invited him up.

Past the altar with the carved wooden crucifix, the crucifix paid for by parish pancake breakfasts where his father and Delancy would tend the grill, his father burning cakes, blaming Delancy, Albert wondering why his mother didn't take over, or why they didn't just pay attention to the food, and Sandy even then talking up the girls. Past the altar, crossing himself, down the corridor to the church's small kitchen, where King's got a scotch broth overheating on the stove.

He turns the soup down, sets the robes on the kitchen table. Doesn't hear Father King anywhere. Sniffs the soup, finds a spoon and dips it in. Grinds in a little black pepper, then a little more, figuring the Father's taste buds must be dull from the smoking. Maybe a little cayenne and Albert's going through the Father's cupboards when he sees the priest out the window, on the parish playground, bouncing a rubber ball toward a five-year-old boy who's crying.

He turns the soup off and covers it.

Albert opens the doorway to the playground, having to put his shoulder to it, wondering how Father King gets in and out. The church more than a hundred years old, built by Irish laborers. His great grandfather had worked on the building. He'd worked on the canals and on the wharves and then he'd gone back to Sligo with no money because he could not stand the heat.

He watches the Father and the boy. The boy bats the ball a couple times, but his heart's not in it, and he gives up, the ball slapping against his small chest. Father King kneels down, looks at the boy, and then gathers him into his arms.

Tears and the boy's nose running, and Albert feeling the heat of the sun off the white stucco walls. Father King whispering, wiping at the small nose with his cuff, the boy's face softening, Father King smiling, and the boy steps from the Father's arms. Turns around in a circle, then again, the boy's shirt rising up his belly, laughing. And Albert feels dizzy, in the heat and the glare, Father King clapping, Hank and Audrey dancing, the smell and softness of her cheek against his own when he lifts her, blue blankets and her hands, the way she'd had him kiss her wet doll, and the boy's pointing to something up in a tree, and Father King's making like it's the most interesting thing that he has ever seen.

Feeling closed in, a shortness in his breath. He suddenly needs air. Negotiating the corridors, avoiding the chapel with its cross and the pews, heading out a sidedoor—he'll mention the robes to Father King at the poker game; he'll light two candles for his da on Sunday—and fast down the empty stone steps, faster across the yard, where he can see Sister Cady, laughing with a classroom of children, two of whom are dressed as sheep.

AT THE DARK Mississippi dockside, a large riverboat, an engine-powered knock-off of a nineteenth-century paddlewheel steamer, lighting up the shore.

Albert, in a beige V-neck sweater and a wide necktie, Chelsea in slacks and an olive blazer, passing along the boat's buffet line that's filled with old couples and out-of-towners.

A Dixie band in the corner of the vast deck room, in red and white seersucker, the whole ship done up riverboat style, draped with red, white, and blue bunting, the meat carvers in suspenders and straw boater hats.

"They certainly don't skimp on the buffet," Albert's

saying, feeling the scratch of his sweater at his neckline, his skin raw and clean from the scrubbing.

She's watching an elderly man dancing, the fox-trot, holding his tiny wife close, their eyes shut, their feet beating the band.

"Hey," Albert continues, "look at that old couple go."

Her plate is sparse: a little beef, a few vegetables, a red potato. His plate is heavy, though not as heavy as he might have liked.

"I'm not much of a dancer myself," he says. "I bet you're light on your feet."

Chelsea smiles softly. "That's a nice thing to say, Albert." Albert nodding. When they'd boarded the boat she'd smiled that same way, quietly, like maybe she was a little tired.

An entire table is dedicated to pie slices and parfait puddings. He's not going to have anything, but then Chelsea takes a red jello, layered fancy with whipped cream, and he takes two pie slices—apple and peach—to be polite.

They sit at a paper-cloth-covered table, along the inside rail, with a view out the window to the dock and the city beyond.

A waitress arrives before he can think of anything to say.

"You have your blue voucher?" the waitress asks.

He pulls the voucher from his wallet.

"That's good for two free glasses of wine," she says. "One each. Or two for one of you. Makes no difference to me."

Smiling. Glances at Chelsea. She's watching the line of taxicabs that light the Quarter edge. Watching them in a way that confuses him, like maybe she does not feel right then that she is even at their table.

"Red or white?" the waitress is asking.

Looking at Chelsea. Not knowing if he should disturb her. On the shore a couple get out of a cab, a young couple, not much older than twenty, and he watches her head turn slightly, following the couple as they head to the river rail, the woman's lips nestled in the crook of the young man's neck.

He turns to the waitress, who's still got her pen on her book.

"It doesn't make any difference to me," the waitress says.

"White," Albert says.

"With roast beef?"

Ship horns wail, Chelsea stiffening, turning to him, she smiles a little and he smiles fully back.

The boat pulls away from the dock. The big spray of water, the blare of horns, smoke where steam once rose, up across the moonlight that cuts a path along the river.

A flower girl passes through the ship's dinner tables, offering a basket of roses. Chelsea and Albert eating silently, a little too silently for his comfort. She'd been quiet all evening, and he has not felt fully himself, not that he was overly talkative, but that he was not able to find too much to say that did not sound dumb. He reaches for his wallet.

Chelsea puts her hand on his, as the girl reaches their table.

"Let me," she says.

"Ah, that's nice," says the flower girl and Chelsea buys him a rose.

Flushing and he knows it and he cannot stop, it is no use to look away. No one's ever bought him a flower before. The rose feels small in his hands. He does not know what to do. Twirls it a little, nodding, finally sniffs it. For a moment, he feels as he did in her bed, the river breeze, the press of her in his arms, the moon and chimes at her bedside, and he takes out his handkerchief and blows so that he might disguise the wetness in his eyes.

She's closer now, her hands near the middle of the table, her arms on either side of her plate. He leans in. He can feel the heat, out from beyond the necklace, from beneath the blazer and her blouse; he can feel now the heat he'd felt in her when she'd an arm across his neck, his hand over hers on the balcony, the softness of her as she slept.

"You're always giving me beautiful flowers, Albert."

Smoothing the red paper tablecloth. "Oh, you got them."

"They were very sweet."

"Yeah, well, maybe the card was a little corny." The river lights across her face and his.

"The card was sweet, too."

He looks away. Out toward a tugboat, cheeks puffing

out, then back, to Chelsea, where he meets her eyes.

"I enjoyed our evening the other night," he says, feeling a trembling in his legs such that he sets his hands in his lap to steady them.

Chelsea laughs. "Oh God, Albert. I should never, ever drink. It's just that, well, Robert had me so upset."

"It was nice hearing about it, about your life and all." He puts his hands back on the table, touches the water glass, the plastic fork, his knife. "I don't have a lot of people I can talk to."

Chelsea nods.

He raises his waterglass. "Well, cheers, Chelsea."

She laughs and she taps his glass with her own. "Cheers, Albert."

He's just got his glass to his mouth when a hand falls heavily on his shoulder, the hand tattooed with H-A-T-E.

"Surprise!" Terry leans against a big woman in a sequined jacket, his girlfriend Dana and they are both drunk.

"Hey, Al! This boat ride seemed such a good idea I figured me and Dana should do it. Sixty bucks, whoa. But look it here—" Terry pulls out a cluster of blue wine vouchers, a couple dropping to the floor. "The guy in the booth knows Bobby Kelly!"

The waterglass is still at his lips.

Dana laughing, Terry leaning against her, wheezing.

Terry juts his chin toward Chelsea. "So this is her, huh, Albert?"

Chelsea seems to smile. "I'm—"

"Chelsea, I know." Terry grins, waves a finger at her. "Fitz can't stop talking about you."

Dana cuffs him. "Terry!"

Terry wraps an arm around Albert's shoulders. Whispers, "Did I tell you pal?" Indicating the boat. "Is this great or what?"

He's unable to get his eyes much higher than Chelsea's hands; staring into the copper bracelet she's twirling around and around her wrist.

"Have you two been out on the deck yet?" Terry's breath is wet into his ear. "You ought to, it's real nice."

She brings a hand to her face and touches her cheek, runs it across her right eyelid, shuts briefly her eyes, the right lid flutters, then sits straighter and curls a blonde hair back behind her left ear.

He feels Terry rapping the side of his head. "Hey, Fitz, you in there?"

"We haven't had a chance yet," Chelsea suddenly says, and she's smiling, only her eyes seem sort of half-closed, like it's suddenly gotten late.

Dana says, "Terry's right. It's real beautiful." He can tell Terry's girl is looking at him, so he nods to be polite. For a moment, no one says anything.

"We should go, Terry," Dana says. "Nice to meet you both."

Terry squeezes his shoulder. "Yeah, see you, Al."

Albert nodding.

"He's speechless," Terry says. "Love struck." Terry gets an idea. "Hey, watch this."

"*Terry*," Dana says.

"He's love—", Terry lightly cuffs him in the jaw with the L-O-V-E fist, "—struck." Terry laughing at his own joke, he forces his lips into a smile that hangs there, his face feeling heavy and gray.

Dana pulling Terry away. "He always does that. Nice to meet you, ah . . . ma'am. See you, Al."

Chelsea's smiling, but he feels like something bad's happened, he can't really meet her face, like he's somehow let her down.

He looks at the half-eaten dinners, the congealed parfait, the cups of thin wine.

"Maybe we should take a little walk," Chelsea says.

She covers his hand with her own.

The tension from Terry falling away.

She stands, he stands; Chelsea puts her arm through his.

"He's not really a bad guy," he says about Terry, clearing his throat, reaching for a little water, the water washing the thickness back into his gut. "He just drinks too much."

He opens the deck door, wishing she would not let go.

"We've all had our moments, Albert."

When she passes, he wipes the dampness from his hands.

. . .

The riverboat gliding along the Mississippi. The breeze, the city lights and the moon. Chelsea's hands are folded at the ship rail. Albert's are straight out from his arms, his right hand inches from hers, his body squared to the water.

"So, you're really in the fish business?"

He thought maybe she'd want to talk about Terry, or maybe about the other night. "Yeah," he says. Feeling his heartbeat; thinking of hers.

She twirls the copper bangle around her wrist.

"You a fisherman?"

"No. My father was. I was never much good at fishing. I sell it." He glances at her. Her face is turned down toward the rail.

"You work with Tommy?"

"Terry. Yeah."

A freighter churns past, slipping downstream.

"I'm supposed to take over for Bobby—maybe you know the place? Bobby Kelly's, it's in the Quarter—you know, when Bobby retires."

He can barely make out her voice, what with the engines and the wake and the wind. "Never been."

"No, well, I guess you get all the fish you need right there in the restaurant."

The freighter gliding by, leaving only rivulets that flatten, then disappear. He takes a slow breath.

"Chelsea, I—"

"I'm going to find the bathroom, Albert." She's suddenly heading for the door. "I'll meet you back inside."

Her face scares him. His breath fast from his lungs, "Maybe we can dance or something?"

"Sure, Albert, sure we can."

He watches her cross the dance floor, sees the kid on the drums, the trumpeter, the guy behind the roast beef, Chelsea hurrying, pushing through a doorway, the doorway swinging back and forth behind her until it is still. The dancing, the hurrying, the plastic beads around Audrey's wrist. The band stops. The husband of the old couple sends his wife into a gentle twirl, her free hand waving in the air.

Coming down the gangplank, avoiding the uniformed captain who's handing out coupons for a future ride, the night is humid and thick, the lights of the docked riverboat float in the heavy air behind them. In front, the far edge of the Quarter.

Albert awkwardly beside Chelsea, among the tourists and the old couples, wanting to take her arm, never finding the right moment. It hadn't seemed much time from when he'd found her sitting outside the ladies' room on a plastic sofa to when the ship had turned around and returned to its dock. They'd danced once, but it was hard to find his footing, not having much experience, and her seeming to always be a step behind the band.

"That was a nice time, Chelsea. A new experience."

He twirls his rose.

She smiles; her expression seems too careful, like maybe it isn't fully real. "Yeah. Albert—"

"We could go for coffee. I never been to that place that's open all night. They say it has great beignets, that is if you're not watching your figure and all." Searching for words. He pats his stomach. "I'm not."

Chelsea laughs, softly. Her eyes seem soft, too, and wide, and they make him smile, cautiously taking her arm in his.

"You know what, Albert?" she says.

Her face close to his now, her green eyes, her smell, the scent he'd try to conjure up when he was alone at work, or in his bed at night, her hair in her face from the wind, remembering it across his lips in her bed with the chimes and the lantern and the heat of her breath at his chest. Albert, his too-round boyish face, the pink skin, the red hair wild, the eyebrows that run every which way. His blue eyes taking her in.

"You are a kind man, Albert. And that's a rare thing."

She shakes her head a little. Her face seems to glide back away.

"A kind, decent man."

She gently releases his arm, takes a few steps from him, toward the darker edges of the dock.

Her smooth neck, the shape of her shoulders, her thin

waist, the shadows of the night and the moon and the shiplights between them. He steps into the dark gap, touches his hand to the small of her back.

"Chelsea—"

She turns. Tears down her cheeks.

And he kisses her, Albert Fitzmorris, just for a moment, straight on the lips.

She presses a hand to his chest. "I should go."

His mind is a whirl: his heart fast and high from the kiss, her words not seeming to match his feelings.

"I'll walk with you," he says.

"No. I'll take a cab. It's a long walk. I—" her voice soft now, too soft, not the voice he knows, "—have to be up, early."

She touches the center of his chest again, gently with the tips of her fingers. "Thanks, Albert." Her fingers against the collar of his sweater, near his lips which feel still warm. Shaking her head, her eyes wet, the night black behind her.

Her walking quickly into it.

She does not turn back. Staring after her, Chelsea disappearing into the shadows, heading toward the Quarter edge, where taxicabs line the shoreline.

"Chelsea—"

The wind blows in from the Mississippi, pulling petals from his rose, lifting them up, drawing them back across the water, dropping them down. Motionless, his lips parted slightly, staring after her, until she is gone.

"Hey, Fitz! Albert!"

Terry and Dana, trailing down the gangplank. Albert walks quickly into the black.

A GRAY DAWN and his ma kneeling in front of the grave: a small, flat marker, one of dozens clustered around a tall Celtic cross, the St. Sebastian's War Memorial, each stone marked by a miniature American flag.

Albert standing behind her, beside Father King, his head bowed, his father's hat in his hands.

"We miss you, Brendan," she's saying. "I miss you. Not a day goes by, I don't think of you." She's pulling out the tufts of grass whose blades have overgrown the marker. "Not a morning comes I don't wish you were beside me. Three years and I still expect to see you every time I open my eyes."

Her voice drops into a whisper; Albert steps away, to give her her visit. Past headstones, past the old tombs with their bodies buried off the ground in defense against the floods. He does not like to see her so small.

Up in a live oak, its branches cut back, its roots hacked away and dug up so that they don't inch into the bodies, he sees two squirrels jumping, and a flock of black birds lining a branch. Behind him, a streetcar rolling past. The car hisses loudly and one bird moves, and then the whole bunch of them move, as if together they had only one mind.

He'd called but she hadn't been in. He'd left a message on her phone answering machine; then called it again just to hear her voice. His ma didn't have a phone answering machine, but he'd left her Bobby's number as well, and Bobby did, though he couldn't expect her to call him as they had only been on two dates never mind the way he feels.

At the edge of the small cemetery, beside the white brick wall, in front of a tomb that's painted blue. Paint not peeling, blue the color of spring sky. A bee's hovering around fall tulips and feeling the sun on his face, watching the bee and the flowers, he feels for a moment at ease.

It's an odd old tomb, not ornate like the ones downtown that people who weren't even family went to visit, though recently people had been getting mugged again. The worn inscriptions, the lettering nearly smooth: an old Italian family, with Antonio, Sr., born 1860 in Palermo. His sons and his daughters, in all there were twelve bodies sealed inside. The last was Rose, and at first he misreads the years of her birth and death such that he thinks she was forty then realizes she was four.

Four, her small body in the black of that tomb, and the flowers outside she would never see, the squirrels chasing each other in the trees. He wonders how a four-year-old girl dies, if she would die like an old man, with tubes and sores, or if she'd died in an accident, swimming, or in a car, or running with scissors the way she'd been taught not to do, or maybe this family did not teach her the right thing, and she'd died because of their failures, alone with no one to watch her. Squinting into the stone, seeing the horse from the balcony and the river below, the girl with the pink balloon, the boy on the shoulders of his grandfather, the grandfather not needing to say a word.

Knowing it is Father King, "Albert?" and looking up hard into the sun, his eyes open such that his vision blurs, breathing in the heat, nodding in respect, and Father King walking toward him.

"You all right?"

"Fine." Then, at Father King's expression, "you know, tired and all."

The Father nods, lights a Pall Mall, smoke up into the trees.

"Those were unfortunate words from Jimmy."

Behind Father King, his mother in her navy dress, the one she wore at the funeral, with the ship anchor buttons, curled over the grave. He suddenly wants to be near her, as if he should be beside her, and when he moves Father King moves with him.

"He's got a good heart, Albert. Jimmy has."

Albert nodding, wishing he could look at the priest, who after all had buried his da, whom he knows is trying to help. Watching his own feet crossing the damp grass.

"I'm sorry, Father."

His ma's done talking, her forehead pressed into the top

of her small, clasped hands. His faint shadow across her and she looks up, Albert lifting her with one arm, the pat of her hand on his shoulder. Joining Father King, leaving him alone with his father.

"Well, Da." He reads the high cross inscription for the hundredth time. "Not much to say. The fish has been good." Dropping to the marker. "You'd be pleased, Da. Speckled trout next month. And the grouper are running like crazy."

Staring. The wind sends the grass back across the grave. He brushes it away, runs his finger in the groove of his own name, Fitzmorris, cold there in the stone.

"Oh, and, um, Elliot Neil took one card."

Nodding; at his father's name, at the big Celtic cross, down at the marker again.

"See you, Da. See you next week."

Crosses himself, joins his mother and Father King who he knows have been talking about him by the way they are silent when he gets there.

Next to his mother on the streetcar, the streetcar moving slowly down the wet New Orleans dawn. Quiet, staring into the morning's grey. He can feel her eyes on him, pressing at the back of his turned head.

"Albert," he hears her say. Turning, his ma's looking down at her hat.

"I was sorry to have missed Audrey's party." She's tugging at the hat's black netting. "Two years in a row now."

She looks up at him and smiles and the smile only makes him feel sicker. "As your father would say, we don't always seem to be aboard the same boat, you and I."

He wants to smile back. His lips feel hard; her face too sad.

"Father King told me you walked out on the poker game."

The train is moving slowly in the rain and he could push past her and out into the street. Instead, he says, "We're through."

He sees his mother slowly nodding. A car honks at a bicyclist who rolls across the neutral ground.

"I see."

Albert's hands grip each other, fingers pressing into the bones.

"Fact is, Ma, Eileen never wanted to marry me."

The wipers of the streetcar sweep wide, from left to right.

His mother wraps his hands in her own.

"So all this time—"

Her eyes remind him of the night when his da came home from Murphy's and finally spoke what they'd all known for months, that the bleeding and the tests did mean he was dying.

"We're just through, all right, Ma?"

Silence again, staring straight ahead, the sweep of the

wipers, the roll of the wheels, the tap of the rain against the tin roof.

"All right."

IN THE BAR across from the Blue Royale Hotel, Albert's drinking a ginger ale. He's got on a topcoat, and he's left his hat at home, so he'd hoped the bartender would not recognize him, but when he got there the bartender was a woman and the old man was no where to be found. He waited at the bar with his ginger ale, giving the bartender a dollar bill tip, until the small table against the bar's window was free.

Sitting there now, he doesn't know why he needs to see her walk down those blue steps, but he will not move until he does. He needs to see her again, with the spire behind her, the blue of the steps against the ivory of her skin, her eyes and the part of her lips, and to know, this time, that she is his, that it was her breath against his skin, that it was her body pressed against his own.

The trumpeter announces himself in the corner stage with a toot-toot. At the table nearest, a big couple, the wife and husband well over two hundred pounds, hold hands and whisper to each other, then laugh so loudly that Albert has to smile, meeting the fat man's eyes, the fat man laughing as if Albert might as well be in on the joke.

Next time when he held her it would be more real still. Next time, he will tell her what he fears to say, what he won't say tonight, and that is that he finds himself thinking of her when he wakes up, and when he goes to sleep, and when he is on the streetcar, downtown, uptown, and when Terry or even his ma is talking to him he is often lost in his thoughts of the lightness of her.

"Chelsea!" He sees her finally come out the brass doors, emerging down the steps in a red dress, a white overcoat, a green rain hat. She does not see him, standing outside in the light of the cracked bar window, across the stone street, nor seem to hear him, so he steps into the road and waves his arms, waiting for a car to pass, then hustling to meet her, catching her at the first, blue step.

"Albert?"

"I thought I could walk with you."

Near her, and he's wearing his da's old topcoat and it is too long on him, and maybe out of style he thinks, but he's had a haircut and a shave with a fresh blade and he's wearing the green sweater that his ma had promised would bring luck when she'd given it to him two Christmases past.

"On account of the other night." Close, in the blue light her skin seems too thin, and he wants to press life into it and she is not smiling, and the brass doors spin on one side of her and the crosses falling away on the other.

"Albert—"

"You know, a rain check."

They will walk along the river.

"I was in the neighborhood."

Her shoulders seem to roll toward him and her face shifts down toward the blue of the steps, until he cannot see her eyes.

"Sure, Albert, sure I'll walk with you." He can barely make out her voice.

He has the walk all planned—maybe he can buy her a cola sno-ball, or even a cocktail if she wanted, and he can watch her green eyes and her smile and listen to her talk.

"So, how was work, tonight, Chelsea?" he asks her, but from the look on her face he realizes this was a mistake, and then he remembers how she did not want to talk about work before. "No," he says, "never mind work, I mean, who cares? Not me." Hands in pocket. Out. In.

As they cross the corner, a guy with a body like a barrel walks toward the bar, the bar window lit from the inside so that all Albert can see is shadows. He thinks for a moment of his father, of his body like a barrel, of how that barrel withered to a stick, how in the end his da had reached out for his hand, and that he did not know what to do so he took it. The skin as rough as a glove, the pinkie nail torn away by the nets, the skin grown over rough, the nail, his da said, sunk to the bottom of the Gulf. And the man turns toward the bar and steps into the glare and is gone and Albert turning to Chelsea and her face is somewhere, too, looking away from him, to the rooftops and a gallery, where two men are holding hands and watching the darkening sky.

"That's sweet," Chelsea says. He tries to draw in her smile, thinking of the way his lips had met hers, the flower she had given him that he had pressed inside his boyhood Bible, and for a minute he is warmed. If it rains they will go to Blanton's where he's noticed that on rainy or windy days they unroll big plastic sheets that protect the riverside terrace without blocking the view.

"I thought we could walk down by the river," he says, introducing this idea sooner than he had planned.

Chelsea stops. She turns to Albert, placing an arm on either of his shoulders. He straightens up and the sky begins to drizzle and she kisses his cheek. It feels somehow wrong. It feels like it did on the riverboat dockside, with her face falling back and his stomach dropping away.

"It's a nice night," he says, and then remembers it is raining and he tries to say something about liking the rain and the plastic sheeting at Blanton's but the look on her face stops him.

"I think I'm going to walk myself home, Albert," she says, and her arms stay on his shoulders for a moment, and then she drops them to her side. "Thank you, though."

She looks at him for a minute, until he has to lower his eyes and when he looks up she has turned from him and is walking away alone.

"Wait—"

A cat pads between them, stopping down the sidewalk, licking its fur against the increasing rain.

He's smiling, but it is not how he feels.

"I thought on account of the other night—" He steps quickly toward her.

"Albert—"

"When we kissed—" His hand is on her arm. She needs to know this, how he feels.

"Let go—"

To hold her, to protect her, to know that she was his. And her face, the green rain hat, the tumble of her hair, her green eyes and they are at once uncertain to him and he realizes how tightly he has been gripping her arm when he feels suddenly the hard tension in his hand.

"Albert—"

He quickly pulls his hand from her. "I'm sorry." Stuffs it in his coat pocket. Finds the bag with the bread in it that if it weren't raining he thought they could toss up to the gulls.

She turns away. "I have to go."

Hand on that bag, squeezing the bread ends, closing shut his eyes.

"Chelsea—"

The back of her coat, the green of her hat, the words he wants to say. The cat follows her, down the center of the sidewalk, and for a moment he thinks of doing the same, only rushing into a cab, beating her to her apartment, waiting for her. That's what Sandy would do, Terry, his da.

And how dumb he is, telling Audrey about fish, not putting her up on his shoulders like that old man in the aquarium, not joining her in her dancing with Hank.

The rain a screen of silver. The cat racing along the park fence, disappearing into a tangle of bushes.

4

He's in the back of Bobby Kelly's, checking the orders for the Delancy wedding. Jimmy having called again to say that he wanted Albert personally to watch over the order, with the wedding just a week away, that Peter, his chef, was nothing but trouble and that he was thinking also lately that Peter was queer, not that it mattered, an issue between him and God, but that everyone knew Bobby Kelly wasn't the same with the orders since his divorce and that's what the single life can do to a man, destroy him one way or the other.

He glances again at the printouts. The orders are basic and there'll be no problem getting Jimmy what he wants: salmon, smoked salmon, oysters, real redfish, lobster tail, and shrimp. Bobby's already lined it up. He'll make a reminder call on behalf of the redfish, which isn't always easy to get at the price Jimmy wants to pay. Even the best boats will take the order, but they can't always fill it.

The doors from the counter swing open.

"Al—get a move on, will ya?"

They've got customers stacked up and more coming in. The doors swing shut.

He should not call her again. He'd left a message at

work and when she wasn't there, he'd left another message at home.

But it may be that she had not got his messages; or that she did not want to phone him at work because she thought he might be busy. He needs her to know that he hadn't meant to upset her by surprising her like that in the rain.

"Hi. We can't answer now. Please leave a message."

The first time he'd heard it, he'd wondered about the "we." But with the crime in the city he understands how she would use "we" on her machine, just as Eileen's mother had once had a tape recording of a dog that she'd play when she heard someone on the stairs. Eileen's machine said "Hank, Audrey, and Eileen," and it strikes him that his mother had never phoned Eileen, or her granddaughter, and heard it.

Or maybe she had. Maybe nothing was news to her. On the streetcar, she'd seemed both surprised and she hadn't. Maybe he was the one in the dark and it was others who knew what was going on.

"Hey, Albert, we've got fish to sell," and this time Terry's holding the doors open, waiting.

He does not know how long it's been since the beep. He punches the off button and gets to his feet. Staring straight to the counter, Terry with an arm to his back, as the door swings shut behind him, to think of nothing but redfish and customers.

• • •

RAIN ACROSS A young couple that hurries down the Fitzmorris' street, the young man creating shelter for the woman with his long beige coat.

Dressing, his skin hot from the shower where he'd again scrubbed it pink, feeling raw now and not clean at all. He'd put in four calls to the Blue Royale Hotel. On the fifth he'd raised his voice.

Fastening his blue slacks, shirtless, avoiding the mirror. Pulls on an undershirt, opens his closet: five white shirts and two blue, two pairs of dark slacks and a pair of dungarees. His father's pullover sweaters. His blue suit. The green sweater on the chair.

Johnny Niles singing of dreams coiling up cigarette smoke.

He pulls a blue shirt from its hanger. The shirt tangles. Tugging it. Stuck. Tugging it a little more, and then he leaves it, tangled in the hanger, slamming shut his closet door.

When his da died they'd gone to Max's to look at suits and they cost then as much as Albert made in two weeks. He'd gone to his father's funeral in his father's altered suit; the same suit he wore on Sundays, the same blue suit she'd

141

seen already twice. If he'd asked his ma, she'd say to buy a new suit at Shaughnessy's, where his father's friends bought their clothes, or maybe at the Clothes Emporium which sponsored the weather report she watched nightly. He did not want blue suits and he did not want white shirts.

When he stepped into the black marble foyer of Max's, he saw himself reflected in the glass, surrounded once more, and it was all he could do to step forward, toward the oak walls, across floors as blonde as she. He'd worn his good shoes, and his newest socks even if they had cost ninety-nine cents at a stand in Jackson Square, and he'd worn the suit blazer over his green sweater in the hopes of appearing casual, but of substance, like he belonged.

He's fingering the material of the suits that hang on an oak wood rack, the pants beneath the jackets, and the shirts and neckties that Albert saw had a price tag for one with piano keys of eighty-five dollars, and he feels the eye of a salesman on him. He would buy what he wanted and put it on the Visa card that he kept in his billfold for emergencies.

"That's a summer suit," says the salesman and he notices that the salesman is about his age, but with hair that combs back and glasses as small as his eyes. "It wears well in the heat," the salesman says as if he could read what was on his mind, Albert gently pulling his belly in, wondering if he was sweating too much, if the salesman could tell how uncomfortable he was. The last time he'd used the charge card was to rent a car when he and his ma had gone to the Gulf on her birthday. She had packed sandwiches and he ate four and they both went in the water even though a sign posted warned of red tide.

"Yes, well, I want something . . . summery. For business. You know, current." The salesman smiles and Albert smiles back, nods. The salesman motions toward a mannequin that's wearing a silvery suit with black stitching along the edge of the lapel.

"It's German. Bosk. Very Berlin."

"Yes."

"We'd have to fit it, though the German suits are meant for a man of substance." He feels his ribs tighten, but the salesman does not appear to be joking. He steps forward and fingers the material. The jacket looks like a cowboy's.

"Is it fashionable?" he asks, and when the salesman begins to laugh he laughs as well until the salesman stops and takes the jacket right off the mannequin.

"You look at this, while I get a, what—48?—from the back."

"Of course."

"And shoes?"

"I can't wear these," and his ears feeling so hot that he yawns and leans his head back. Up at the ceiling, a chrome ball with camera lenses stares back and he looks away and fingers the material some more, thinking he could leave, but staying.

In the shoe section beside the suit racks, a short, stern man with a low brow in a brown suit seems to be watching him and he remembers the Blue Royale Hotel dick and he fingers the material of the suit jacket more vigorously until it feels hot in his hand. He holds a sleeve up to the light, nearly sniffs it, the piano music overhead into a tune he recognizes but cannot name and when he lowers the sleeve the suit salesman is waiting.

"I've got it," the salesman says, smiling. The salesman extends his hand and Albert almost takes it.

The salesman holds open a wood-slated swinging door and he steps into a dressing room to be met by the German suit hanging from a mahogany hanger on a brass hook. Feeling hot in the sweater and the coat, and when the salesman steps into the dressing room behind him, the salesman's smile floats in the mirrors around Albert's head.

"Let's try it on," says the salesman, and he takes Albert's jacket off. "The Bosk is a very original suit." Albert pulls off his V-neck sweater and when the salesman continues to stand there he unbuttons his dress shirt as well.

"It's got attitude."

He supposes maybe it does: the silver material looks like metal, a metal cowboy jacket. He certainly does not look like a guy who would sit in the pews of St. Sebastian's.

"And authority."

"And this is an up-to-date suit? I mean, not just anyone would wear this, not to church, of course?"

The salesman laughs in a way that again feels like they have been friends and the salesman says, "No, you wouldn't wear that suit to church."

He nods.

"And look at this," the salesman reaches into the hanging suit and removes a black pullover jersey that he hadn't noticed. "It's silk," the salesman says as if they are sharing a secret.

He slips out of his dress shirt. The salesman's on about Milan when he hears the salesman's voice catch briefly and he realizes that the undershirt he has on is not the new one he'd laid out, but instead is an old one, torn along the sides and stained beneath the arms.

He turns from the salesman and quickly pulls the jersey over his head.

His head almost doesn't come through the jersey's collar, popping out, the collar scratchy around his neck, the silk shirt clinging to his belly like skin. Runs a finger along the tight cuff of the right sleeve. Looking at himself in the mirror, turning to the salesman.

"Perfect," the salesman says.

Albert not so sure, what with the scratching and the clinging and the black, like it was a shirt for a different kind of person. His fingers in the cuff, tight, and a price tag slides out and he looks at it and the shirt costs $168.

Albert glances at the suit, then at the salesman, then back at the mirror, the mirror falling away such that Albert turns his back from it and leans against the wall.

"I'll take it," he says. The salesman smiles. "The shirt. And the suit—I'll come back for the suit. It's late. I didn't realize."

"So we'll ring up the suit and schedule an appointment for alterations?"

"The shirt." Ears burning, white talc on the hem of the silk.

"Just the shirt?"

Not meeting the salesmen's eyes.

"I see."

"Until I have more time."

"Of course."

SHE HAD NOT returned his calls. The rain sheeting now, across the wide glass wall of the Blue Royale Room. He should not have raised his voice, so he'd be certain she'd got his messages. He would wait; he would make with her again a proper date, not spring out at her from the rain.

He knows already that the shirt was a mistake. He does not feel right in it, the material tight against his chest, and the blue suit coat making him hot with no shirt buttons to undo. He considered not wearing the shirt after all, but then he remembered that what he thought was right was not necessarily so, that he was somehow behind Chelsea, that a place like Max's went better with a place like the Blue Royale Hotel. He would leave himself open to new things, improve himself.

It was Friday. She said she worked the weekends. He knew she was busy. He would wait at the bar until she showed up and then he would propose a future date, and then he would leave her to her work.

Facing the empty foyer, drinking a ginger ale.

The barman to his side. "A refill?"

Albert turns, glances at his half-finished soda.

"No charge for soft-drinks," the barman says, topping up his glass.

Watching the couple across the bar, the ease of their conversation, the comfort of their bodies even as they're pressed close.

"Carly," the barman indicates a waitress who's setting waterglasses onto the empty tables, "she says she doesn't think Chelsea's working tonight, but as I say, I'm filling in, so I can't say for sure." The lights from the Quarter bend through the rain as it flattens along the window glass. The trio warming up.

Nodding.

"But Carly, she says Chelsea's not on the schedule."

Laughter. And for a moment his eyes almost make the small, older hostess into her.

The lights of the streetcar and the Quarter, the slide of the notes from the bass, the scar on his finger from the boats when he was twelve. Cutting a fish for bait, the boat rolling, the knife edge sticking into the skin of his knuckle. His thumb to the scar, and he can still feel the blade. And he can still feel his father wrapping the finger in gauze, Albert showing the blood stain like a badge to his brother, his ma kissing it, then Sandy kissing it, and finally his da making like he was going to kiss it and everyone laughing; and his da's fingernail at the bottom of the Gulf, the nail inside a fish inside a fish inside a fish.

The trio's drummer yawning; the wet cough of the man on the sax. Chelsea's breath across his chest was filled, it was, with wine.

He tries to make his voice sound upbeat. "Maybe—"

The woman's fingers to the collar of the man's red shirt. Eileen clutching her knees at the foot of the live oak. The spin of the carousel. And earlier, the walk they'd taken, Eileen crying in the park, to tell him, and there were Christmas lights, and a drunken Santa, and staring up to those lights, he thought of the baby Jesus, and his own baby now, the blessing that would be Audrey, and, he was soon to know, the sadness in it. She would not marry him. He could not expect it. His ma and Sandy at the table with Delancy and Elliot Neil.

The light from four candles on Audrey's small face.

She may have bookkeeping to do. That would bring her

in. She may come in to supervise this other hostess. Or to talk with the hotel manager about her schedule, maybe planning to take that trip to her mother's wedding after all.

"Maybe—" raising his glass, "—maybe I'll have a small whiskey, after all."

The towering spray of flowers. The pink cupids of the foyer dome.

IT WAS ELEVEN when he'd left the bar, the wet alley, his shoes slick, his jacket heavy and damp against his skin. He will not run. If he ran it would be like a fisherman carrying too much bait; it would call in the bad. When his da had cried out for his own mother, who had died before Albert was born, Albert had run to get his ma and when they came back he was gone. Storm clouds lit up over Albert's head, up above Friday night partiers in the long windows behind the French Quarter balconies, music sweeping out to the street.

He's watching the balconies, trying to remember.

His shoe slides across a flattened go-cup, stumbling, clutching at the paper bag he's got pressed to his chest, beneath his coat, trying to keep it dry. He may have missed a turn, but then he finds the begonias above the steps where he once felt warm and clean.

He stands in the light of her entranceway. The bag is

wet and he pads at it with his hands and some of the paper tears away. He brushes back his hair. He extends his right hand toward the four buttons of the old intercom. Its edges blur.

He rings her but she does not answer. Staring at the button, the rain coming down harder now, spraying out the cracked pipe that runs the length of the entranceway, pouring down just beyond his feet.

He presses the button again.

He wipes at his face with his sleeve. Maybe she is ill. Or maybe she just didn't feel like going into work. The day after his da's funeral he hadn't gone into Bobby Kelly's, he'd walked down by the river instead.

When it comes, her voice startles him, bursting out from the speaker, asking a question as if it knows the answer. *"Who's there?"*

Sounding harsh and far away.

"Hello?"

"Hi. Chelsea—"

"Oh, Albert." The way she says this makes him feel sicker. *"You shouldn't have come."*

The front door glass is cold against his cheek. "I've brought you a present."

He holds the bag to the speaker. The alcove dips and he pulls his face from the glass.

"Go home, Albert." Her voice sounding smaller and smaller. *"You really, really should just go home."*

"Chelsea—"

"I've got to go."

And he buzzes and there is no reply.

"Chelsea—"

No answer. Buzzes. Nothing.

His chest begins to heave and he feels he cannot breathe.

He pounds the speaker that has cut her from him.

"Chelsea!"

Pounding with his fist, harder and harder, "Chelsea—Chelsea—Chelsea—" until the steel grate dents.

"CHELSEA—"

Out in the stone street, her name bursting from him.

"CHELSEA—CHELSEA—" he trips on something, the curb, to his knees, pain in the back of his head, his silk shirt staining, staring up to the balcony, tearing the skin of his palms.

"CHELSEA—"

The balcony's french doors open. The blue light of a television angles off the top of the glass. To him, from the street, she seems to rise from the flowers: her gold hair, her soft face, her shoulders in a white shirt, the gold at her neck, the drape of the collar to her chest.

Wet and kneeling in the street. He finds her eyes.

"Why won't you call me, Chelsea?"

"Albert . . . "

Standing, wiping at his elbows and at his knees. "I

called you. You're never home. You said . . . you said you worked in the morning . . . And at nights. I waited for you. I waited Chelsea, I waited for you."

"Albert, get off the street."

"I WAITED FOR YOU." He hears his own voice, loudly around him. For a moment it is as if it belongs to someone else. He finds the paper sack in his hands and he holds it up to her.

"I brought you this."

The bag sliding beneath his fingers, wet; he peels it away from the big book inside, dropping the paper into the street.

"It's the best one they had. Because you can think about going, Chelsea. We can plan it." Holding the book up to her at the end of his arms as if she might reach down and take it. *The Islands of the Caribbean*, the cover showing a white beach in Montserrat. His hair across his face, pushing it from his eyes, smiling slightly, he was happy when he'd found it, his blue suit heavy against the black shirt and his skin.

Rain down her cheeks and then he thinks that maybe she is crying.

"Chelsea?"

He can't hear her, but he can see her lips trembling and her head softly nodding, her face looking into the flowers.

"Because there's lots for us to do, Chelsea. I could take over Bobby Kelly's if you wanted me to." The rain's falling all over the opened book, and he wipes it, not wanting to take it from her view. "And I could buy a boat, because you said you liked the water."

He can just make out her words. "You have to go, Albert."

And the page tears and he's wiping it with his sleeve and he stares to her, blinking as the raindrops fall into his eyes.

"You just have to go."

He feels his head nodding, feels the smile heavy in his lips.

He finds himself talking. "I know I'm not a great catch, Chelsea. I'm fat. People won't sit next to me because I stink of fish."

Staring up to her eyes, his words all around him.

"But, your hand felt right in mine. And I took your smile with me, when I went to sleep, Chelsea, when I went to work in the morning."

The lights of the television shift against the glass doors behind her, bluer still.

"I thought you liked me, Chelsea. I thought maybe you and me . . . "

The man that rises behind her, stepping through the french doors, his shirt undone, is like the Jaguar man only heavier, and the gold of his watch band catches in the light of the street as he reaches for her.

"I do like you Albert," she's saying.

And the whole alleyway reels, her balcony sliding below the one beside it.

He hears her, "No. William. Go inside," and then he hears his name, and hears it again, echoing around him, and again, chasing him as he runs.

Albert bursting through the broken front doorway, the remaining rusted hinge bolts of the steel security door snapping, charging up the thin wood stairs, missing a step, his shin slamming, momentum unbroken, rushing her door and pounding it with his hands.

"EILEEN!"

Pounding.

"EILEEN!"

Eileen opens the door, in a Shadowland's T-shirt, rubbing at her eyes. "Albert?"

Knocking her with his shoulder, past her, dizzy, turning round and round in the living room.

"Jesus, Albert."

"Where is she?"

"Take it easy."

He swings open a door. The kitchen. Turns, charges across the flat, remembering the bedrooms ran off the short hall.

"ALBERT!"

"AUDREY!"

Hank there suddenly, arms folded against his bare chest.

"Where's my daughter?"

Moving low, drunk, he reels hard toward Audrey's door,

Hank shifting in front of him as Albert lunges for the knob.

"Take it easy, Albert."

"Get out of my way."

Hank blocking the door.

"I won't do that, Albert. Just sit down. We'll get you some coffee."

Breathing hard, just that sound, all through his head, and his shoulders dropping, like he might fold down to the rug.

"Come on, Al," Eileen says, "come have some coffee."

"You won't see me. I'm her father."

"I know that Albert."

"You don't remember."

Folding over, so that if he wanted his arms might touch the ground.

"Albert—" And her voice is soft, like she is talking to a child.

"I'm her father, not him. You and I—" And charging, full force at Hank, hitting him low around the midsection, them crashing into Audrey's closed door.

Hank yelling, his arms around Albert's neck, twisting it. "Don't do it, Albert," forcing him toward the living room.

Albert's arms swinging hard, his fists beating Hank's ribs. A lamp crashes.

"AUDREY!"

He turns his body and smashes Hank's beard with the butt of his elbow. Hank's head snaps back. Hank roars, lifts Albert off his legs, the two men falling backward and

Hank slamming Albert against the living room wall.

Eileen rushes at them. "Stop it, Albert. Both of you, stop it, stop it, stop it—" Eileen shoved from the fight, falling into the center of the room, and Audrey's in her doorway, in musical note pajamas, holding the Madeline doll across her chest.

"Mommy—"

Audrey rushes into the living room as he kicks away from the wall, to see her, to see her, Hank with his hands still at his waist, Eileen screaming as Albert swings wildly at Hank, the two men spinning, out of control, lunging toward her, swinging at Hank, feeling his elbow hard against the side of something too soft and too small.

Eileen to her knees, pressing her daughter into her body.

In the middle of the room, staring at his daughter, at the blood running from her mouth, her too surprised to cry.

"Audrey—"

"GET OUT. Get out, get out—" Eileen crying into her daughter's hair, Hank leaning on the wall behind him, Hank's head pressed against it.

"Oh, God, Albert just get out."

And Audrey starts to cry and he steps toward them.

"GET OUT!"

Falling toward the hall.

• • •

ALBERT, FACE BURSTING, busts out of the broken doorway and blindly into the night. Rain falling still, Albert down the middle of the road.

"Audrey!"

A car swerving, honking— "Audrey!"— disappearing.

"I didn't mean it. I didn't, I didn't."

The steady rain, the city reflected around him.

A couple makes a wide path; his clothes torn, blood across his mouth and shirt.

"Audrey—"

Headlights again, a car from the front, horn blaring, falling toward the curb. His hands do not break his fall. The underside of his forearms hit against the stone.

Music and he's fighting for breath, swallowing, and blood. Four balconies above his head are strung with banners, "It's!—Bula's!!—Birth!!!—Day!!!!"

Balconies filling with couples, music and laughter spilling into the rain.

He opens his mouth to yell. But nothing comes. A car, water splashing up from its tires, then back down to the pot holes and the tar.

Staring into the black night. Bleeding and rain, and he pulls his knees to his chest. A burning through every pore, and wet in his eyes. The laughter swells from the galleries above, toy horns sounding, and the singing, *Happy birthday, dear Bula.*

And the blackness comes, spilling out from his lips,

coughing it up, the violence in his lungs, the silk shirt torn, the blackness a dark gush from his insides to the stones.

Above him, from off the balconies, bead necklaces and party ribbons stream into the night, purple and yellow and green, a whole block's worth, falling across Albert with the rain.

5

An old man pulls a wagonfull of cans down the wet potted street, the cans rattling as the clouded sun rises through the white oaks and the palms. The noise of cans like kicks to his body, Albert rolling his face away from his opened shade.

His ma's tapping on the bedroom door, his face burning as he turns it. Tapping louder, "Albert!" And knocking now, "You haven't slept this late since you were fifteen. Albert!"

The bedroom door opens, she comes through carrying a tray. "I made you breakfast, lad, for a change."

The shades never drawn, his clothes everywhere, he knows his face is bad from the look that's suddenly in her eyes. "My God." She sets the tray to the dresser and presses a hand to his face.

"It's not as bad as it looks." His eyes feel punched. He wets his lips, tastes blood cracked and dry. He forces a smile. "It was all a big accident."

"Did you get the number of the truck?"

Difficulty opening his right eye. With the left, staring into the folds of his mother's brown dress.

She pulls the black shirt from the tangle of bedclothes. The rips and the dirt and the blood. The silk and the Italian label. She just holds it.

"So. Your breakfast is on the dresser." Her lips go thin. "I have to get over to the parish, something to do with the Father's wedding chasuble. You've done a job on this shirt. And what sort of shirt is this?"

"I can't go."

Her lips part and then they tighten again. She carries the tray to his bedside.

"Stay in bed a little longer." She touches his arm. "But I did promise Jimmy you'd help King with the chairs and the heavy lifting."

"I mean tonight." He does not look at her. "I can't. Tonight."

"To the rehearsal dinner? Don't be silly, Albert. We're sitting with Jimmy—at the head table. Albert look at me!"

He's not sure why the tears are there, now, when all seems to be finished, but the wet allows both eyes to open and to see. Her bright eyes dull, the sag at her neck and her shaking. And he rolls away from her, from the breakfast at the bedside and the memory of his ma small at the graveside and the failure that he is.

"I can't."

"You must."

"I won't."

In the front room, the telephone is ringing.

"Albert," is all his mother says.

• • •

He hears her; lying there, the light from the window and the photographs and even the smell of coffee sickening to him.

"Surely you didn't . . . surely he didn't. Oh, Jimmy! Not your new chef—" Delancy. He needs to get up, to go to the bathroom where he is not sure he won't be sick again.

"He'll be back, Jimmy. He can't do this to Kara."

Throwing off the bedspread, lifting his chest and his head. The bedroom door dips way down. The room heaves. He shuts his eyes; red lights stream across the black. The alley. His knees throb. Her lip.

"Not on the day before the wedding."

In his briefs and one sock that is brown, and he puts one foot in front of the next, his ma in his da's big chair, and closing the bathroom door when he gets there, shutting out his mother's voice, finding the john where he sits, his face in his bruised hands.

SHE HADN'T BEEN back even for lunch. When he'd lifted his head again from his bed, it was four, and the house was hot from the sun.

He'd carried the breakfast tray to the sink, having had the coffee cold, searching for aspirin in the medicine cabinet but finding only his Old Spice, witch hazel, and talc. She normally took half an aspirin with breakfast, but the bottle beside the kitchen window was empty. Out the window, three dogs, collielike, were racing down the street, biting at each other's necks. The barking up into his eyes; the sun long against the still damp blacktop.

She kept her evening pills at her bedside, that's what brought him to their room. Beside the pill tray was a wooden box. The box had been on their bedside table for as long as he could remember. It was from Doolin, her hometown, his father had arranged it with her sister who like her brother had now passed on. With knots interweaving, at the top a crown and the singing bird of happiness. It was filled with nicknacks, stuff that had meaning only to them. Normally he noticed it no more than the table it sat on.

He'd set the aspirin down and opened the lid.

And inside: a baby picture, her or maybe his father, in black and white, cracks through it like netting; and his da in a rocky field, outside Knightstown where Albert's grandfather was born, on the trip his parents had taken to Ireland when Albert was four, Albert staying with Delancy and Delancy's wife who'd died when Albert was six; peat fires burning in the stone houses, his da in a wet rain slicker, round face smiling and wide, his da holding onto a goat.

Of Albert with Sandy on a pony in City Park; Sandy alone in his band uniform; communion and Sunday dinner; a picture of Albert when he'd made the trip with his ma two years ago to the sea—he's got a sandwich to his mouth, and he realizes how pale his ma had then looked, in the color photo from his da's Polaroid, a year after his da's death, her hair thin and her face so that you could nearly see her bones.

A ticket stub from a VFW dance at the Crescent City Local. Two stubs from the Lake Ponchartrain Zipper.

His da's wedding ring.

And a note that he opened and read, the creases transparent from use.

August 17, 1950

Dear Dori,

You great git.

Sincerely,

Brendan Fitzmorris, Himself

He stands in the middle of the silent shotgun house, straddling the line between the kitchen and the darkened front room. The telephone where she left it. Her bowl, damp with milk. His father and the pope on the wall. Sunlight through the kitchen, warm on his back, a box of light across the wooden floor. And his body black inside it, black across the throw rug and the chair. A shadow, black, in this light.

For a minute he is on the streetcar with the heat against his neck, staring into the ad above his head; and then the couple on the LP cover comes clear: the two lovers, the man's black face smiling, the woman's white coat twirling, *The Thing is Love*, them not caring about the onlookers or the rain.

The scratched hi-fi. His da's empty chair. And her Singer, the guide light still glowing, draped with his own daughter's dress.

By five he had dressed. He'd done his best to cover the cuts on his face, and he'd been sick once straight into the toilet, and then his head had felt more clear.

He is surprised to find the Chop House kitchen empty, on the eve of the wedding, noise rolling in from the dining room, and then he remembers the conversation his ma had had on the phone with Delancy. Delancy's chef had quit; Delancy getting what, at least, should have come as no surprise.

Passing the big stoves, quiet now, only the glow of the pilot lights. Past the door to Delancy's office, thinking of Delancy's hand to his face, treating him like he was a boy. A fluttering from behind the poker room door; the game table's covered with food. Crates of tomatoes and pears, jars of red peppers, bags filled with cake flour and bread. A label loose and flapping against the bushel of red cabbage in the chair that was once his father's. Floating in the current from the fan.

The voice of Topper O'Brien, calling out Elliot Neil's name, and the shouts of children playing. He sees them as if they are there. Elliot Neil and Father King. The Father on the playground with the boy. The photograph of Delancy as a boy, the stern, Irish faces; Audrey, newborn, in his arms, the nuns calling Eileen Mrs. Fitzmorris, Albert not setting them straight; Topper, caught in an ear-wiggling scheme with Elliot Neil, two for a pair, three wiggles for three of a kind, Topper confessing to Father Tim, Father Tim keeping the oath of confession for as long as it took him to call Albert's da. Delancy and his da wiggling their noses the Saturday next, sending Elliot Neil into a panic.

And Delancy retelling that story from his father's big chair, sitting up all night with Albert, at home, that night when his da, for the first time, was not thinking clearly, was dreaming when awake, Delancy with one story after another, about the merchant marine, about the time Topper bought a parakeet to put over the dart board at Murphy's so his da might stop throwing high, about Delancy's own boyhood off Jackson Avenue, his mother and his wife, and when his ma emerged from her room, claiming that she'd slept, it was Delancy who made the breakfast of red pepper, eggs, and fried bread.

His hand on the back of his father's chair. Crimping the tops of the bread bags. Red cabbage and pears. Shutting down the fan.

He stands before the green dining room door and with a breath he swings it open. Voices and laughter roll across him such that for a moment he steps back. Tables in the formation of a diamond. Father King, laughing with Elliot Neil's wife, her back curled over from bone loss, the Father leaning up against a wall. Elliot Neil at a table just to his left, with Topper, their backs to him, Topper with a drink raised toward a young man Albert does not recognize, the young man speaking into Topper's better ear. And he sees Kara, with her fiancée, moving from table to table, holding hands, happy. People swapping chairs, arms around necks, wine pouring and stories. Scanning the room for his ma.

A line of children rushes past. A snake of clasped hands, winding through tables and misplaced chairs. Sister Cady in the middle, she's got on a hat, and then the tail of the snake breaks free and a little girl spins, spinning across gold scrolls of carpet, twirling past Delancy and his ma.

She's carrying a stack of dinner plates toward a buffet Delancy's set up at the back of the room. Whispering to each other. Grey, hushed against the laughter and the talking. Delancy's hands move violently, Delancy on a tear, cannot stand still, would not have stood still, Albert knows, since he phoned her. His ma nodding, a hand to Delancy's arm. She will not have eaten. Her eyes seem heavy. The food in the poker room. Her bringing his breakfast to him on a tray.

And suddenly his ma's eyes widen. Delancy stands quickly straighter. Kara there, taking her grandfather's hand.

Kara says something, her smile, and she's laughing into

Delancy's ear, an arm up around his neck. Delancy is rigid and his eyes are past her, he is studying the buffet in a way that Albert understands: he's told his granddaughter nothing. She shakes him around a little. Delancy closes his eyes.

And Delancy's made a horseshoe pit among the roots of the trees behind his old home, and Sandy's no good at it, but Delancy's got a hand on Albert's back, and he's guiding him, his first throw hit the clothesline but his second leaned up against the stake, you've got the knack, Albert Fitzmorris, Brendan he's got the knack, his da grinning, the rusty shoe up again into the air, their shirts off in the sun.

Kara cuffs Delancy once to the belly. Delancy's face softens. Kara whispering something else to him, and then Delancy's smiling, and Kara's got his chin in her hands, and he's laughing, and Delancy's grabbed a fork from the buffet, and he's poking at her. Kara in a gold dress. Delancy with an arm to each of her shoulders. His hands clasped behind her neck. The children dancing past. Delancy's eyes squeeze shut. Audrey on the carousel. And how it was different.

He thinks of her lip. His elbow swinging as if on its own, the hush of her body against the rug. His own flesh. And then he sees again his ma. She's turned back to the buffet, Delancy and Kara behind her, and she's smoothing the buffet's table cloth, sweeping loose crumbs from the table to her palm.

All his hiding. And what it has brought him. Alone in

the doorway in his da's blue suit.

He steps toward them. To be beside her. To help Delancy with the buffet. And then he stops. No one has seen him. He knows what he must do, what he can do. He turns quickly, shoulders the swinging door.

He rushes back across the Chop House kitchen.

He'll explain it all later, on the phone, it would take too long now, to say what he just barely understands, and he's outside, and the sun's setting, and Delancy's loading dock door's just slammed behind him when he bounces it back open, and hurries to the poker room, for the snow peas, the red peppers, the tomatoes, and the bread.

IT'S 9:00 P.M. IN THE Fitzmorris kitchen and it would've been even later had Bobby not personally lined up the purchases, and Tommy Alfieri, coming in from Metairie to help him, and now it was nine and he'd had more coffee than he'd normally have in a week. Phoning his ma, and it's the twenty-second ring, and he'll wait until someone breaks from the rehearsal dinner and passes by the phone.

He hopes it won't be Delancy.

"Delancy's Chop House." He can barely hear the voice with the clatter of voices.

"Hello."

"Yeah, we're closed."

"Jimmy?"

"Who's this?"

He cannot face him and he doesn't have the time. There is too much to say and there is not time to say it and he's got four pots boiling and suddenly there's a little too much smoke coming out the sauté pan.

"Sandy Fitzmorris," Albert says.

"Sandy! Jesus, Sandy I'm sorry you couldn't make it, but what with work and all. Still, your brother, that's another story—"

"Can I just speak with my ma then?"

"He's broken her heart."

"Let me talk with her—"

"He's no good. Your brother, he's become a no good—"

Albert burns his hand, dropping the phone, the receiver dangling around the hot stove, and then snatching it up and hearing his own voice be quick again, ideas popping in him, and though it's a lie he hears himself say, "fire—FIRE," yelling, "I gotta run, get the hoses, get my ma, quick, FIRE—"

"—village idiot. Ah! Fire! Shit! OK, hold the line, Sandy, hold the line—".

The Fitzmorris kitchen crowded with bag after bowl of food.

When his ma gets on, he'll tell her and Jimmy what he has done.

• • •

BUTTER SPITTING from the sauté pan, pan's too hot, but he's just taken onions from it, no time to cool down; water boiling for poaching in the big pot, tossing in salt, working fast over the counter of snow peas; it's four in the morning, cutting, peeling, timers for two pots of crab claws ding.

Neil Diamond rolling loud, five salmon nearly finished, his ma and the Sisters stuffing, chopping; knives flying, music swinging, the big pots boil and steam.

"Eight hours," Father King announces from the table, hovering over the row of poached salmon that's longer than he, layering toast rounds, fast, fast, studying his wedding sermon from the Bible he's set beside the fish. "Eight hours till noon."

Albert doesn't look up from the snow peas. "There's a wedding for fifty finished—"

"One hundred to go."

"God'll help us," Sister Cady says and she hurries a tray toward the fridge.

His ma bringing a bottle of whiskey.

"And that," says Father King.

The snow peas blurring, Albert cracking crab shells with his bare hands, shredding horseradish for the shrimp in his head.

• • •

Radio news out the kitchen window, late morning sun now streaming in. A couple jogging, pushing a baby stroller done up in ribbons and pinwheels, the baby screaming with glee.

The kitchen; every inch an hors d'oeuvre. Thousands across every plate and pan and table space. The refrigerator pumping icy air, the door forced open by the overflow inside. Every surface slick with vegetable ends and grease.

His ma sleeping in her dress in the big chair, a steel bowl of strawberries in her lap. He wipes the cold water from his face, splashes it again, his lips still sting, the dark bruise around his eye, breathing warm air from the street.

Waiting for the shrimp to cook pink.

Glancing at the clock he's tried to avoid.

It blurs, then focuses.

Fifteen minutes and then it will be noon.

Staring into it, watching the second hand go slowly round. He remembers the clock in the maternity ward waiting room, with his ma knitting in the corner, each passing swipe bringing him closer to the miracle. And further back, the day he and Sandy came home from school at St. Sebastian's when his ma had been in the hospital for one night, just for a check-up his parents had told him, and his da saying there was a dollar for each of them on his dresser, and rushing to his parents' room to find her, home in their bed, and not knowing why they were so happy, and she having to blow her nose into a tissue, their da in the doorway, arms folded and smiling.

They never talked about it, about why his ma had gone to the hospital at Tulane, but they never had a younger sister or brother, his ma telling Colleen that God had limited her gifts to two, so Albert and Sandy figured they knew.

The front door buzzes.

Albert claps his hands, his ma jumps up, strawberries tumble across the floor, the Sisters rushing from the two bedrooms, no one knowing they'd been sleeping.

"What time is it?" his ma says. "Fifteen minutes? Oh, Albert we'll never make it."

Pulls the shrimp from the burner, rushing past her to the door that's buzzing, buzzing. He slaps her knee. "We'll make it."

He throws open the front door.

Five firemen storm the shotgun kitchen.

The ambulance's screaming through the uptown streets, sirens wailing, lights blazing. Inside, food everywhere: big trays strapped to the stretchers, his ma's silver wedding platters piled across heart machines, stainless bowls and oven racks stacked along the walls. Albert's trying to maintain the mountain of boiled shrimp he's got piled into two fire hats, the ambulance careening hard around a turn.

Up front, his older brother's got the pedal to the floor.

"Step on it, Sandy-boy," his ma's urging, pressing down on her eldest son's leg, "Don't let your old mother down!"

TOM DOOLEY AND the Dooley Dance Band are swinging a storm on the ballroom's bandstand. Beneath the chandeliers that hang from the domed ceiling, out across the polished floor, his ma and Jimmy Delancy are dancing as if it were 1950. And Delancy's granddaughter and her groom behind them, spinning in their youth.

Albert at the dwindling buffet table, refilling a small plate twice. He'd fallen asleep at the service, his ma nudging him only when he'd snored, mostly just holding his hand in her own.

A friend of the groom's biting into a crab ball. "The food's been delicious," he says to his date.

"Outstanding," she says. "If a little heavy on the fish."

Grinning. Thinking the ginger root toasted well, didn't dry out, he'd sprayed it twice with water; noticing that all his pink shrimp were eaten, wondering how the guests liked the horseradish because it was fresh, figuring they did because the bowls of his sauce were also nearly gone. A snow pea on the tablecloth. His design of a clover for luck is long lost, the snow peas scattered across the tray. With a toothpick he straightens them, so that they at least form circles out from the center. He glances at the couple, who aren't looking, and spears the snow pea from the table cloth, popping it with a crab ball into his mouth. He's been hungry all day.

Watching his ma and Jimmy Delancy. The ease they had together. And Sandy and Colleen, her belly big between them. And even Father King, alone with his nervous smoking, the generosity King found in himself, for Albert, for the parish students, for Albert's dying father. What was put into practice; God in life crowning the God in words.

When he sees her, he closes his eyes twice to make sure that she is real. She's across the floor, on the far edge, in front of an open alcove, watching the couples dance. He turns before she can see him. It is too sudden. He does not know why she is here. He thought he would approach her first by telephone, or wait for her mother to call, and he feels himself shaking, his body shivering in the midst of the heat. And then he turns back, raising his face to her and when she disappears behind a twirl of dancers, he's suddenly scared that she is gone. Pushing onto the dance floor, chandelier lights swirling, the blur of the couples, the dancers like the fans in that French Quarter bar, stealing his air, and so close to the river where he could walk, but the river lights and the ship horns will remind him.

He could stand in the dark street behind the hall, alone and with nothing, where he could breathe again, and no one would know that he was missing.

Instead, he takes another step in her direction.

His heart beating thickly inside his da's blue suit. She's holding the hem of her white dress, swaying softly from side to side. Each footfall felt, in and out of the dancers. He wants to fold her into his arms.

And then he sees again her busted lip.

Audrey does not notice him, and then she does. A smile that falls fast, the dark scabs at her lips reminding them both of what he has done.

He steps from the edge of the dancefloor.

"Hey." An arm's reach from her. "Hey, Aud."

"Hi."

In the small space between them he kneels, his left knee into the floor. His head bowed, knee throbbing, pushing his leg hard into the tiles.

Say something and he does.

"You want to hit me back?"

He looks up at her. She shakes her head. He looks away.

"Your father . . . " He pauses until he is able to say this meeting her eyes. "Your father, me, well, I was really stupid."

Audrey nods.

"I never want to hurt you, darling."

And his face into tears, his hands on his knee, not covering his face, but keeping it raised to her, tears falling thickly off his chin, never turning from his daughter's wide eyes.

The horns blast and the band's into something fast and

behind her there's Eileen, in the big arched doorway, in bluejeans and Hank's leather jacket. She nods at him, and then she gently smiles.

ALONE NOW IN the Fitzmorris kitchen and it's midnight. Moonlight through the window, passing over the stacks of dishes and pans and bowls and utensils that pile out the sink, along both countertops, and onto and across the kitchen table. In his apron, the tape recorder playing a slow Irish fiddle, Albert filling bag after bag with trash. He's been up, by the clock, for forty-six hours. When he'd said good night to his ma, she'd kissed him straight on the lips. He'd thought about this. Thirty-five years old and he could only get his own ma to kiss him. Shaking his head. Maybe he'd ask Colleen to fix him up. She'd offered. He was not maybe terrible to look at, and he was not the type to run around.

He hears barking from out near his step and he thinks of the stray, on her watch in the neighborhood where no one lets her in. He's got the corned beef steamer full of scraps for her, so many that he'll have to keep some in a bowl in the freezer. He'd once seen that dog go after two kids who were beating up a boy; by the time he'd gotten outside the stray had chased them off and was gone.

It was enough to have told Audrey his wrong. He

wished they had danced on the dance floor, beneath the chandelier, with his mother and his parents' friends. He would call Eileen when he was rested. He hadn't said much to her at the wedding. They hadn't stayed long. Just for Audrey to see the wedding, Eileen'd said. He would call her and he would have planned what it was he wanted to say. He would present himself for Audrey. If Hank were in Audrey's life then he would know him. She was his own daughter, despite what even the church might sometimes say.

The knock on the door's so light that he thinks it's the cassette tape ending. When the side with the ballads comes round again and he hears the knock once more, his eyes move to the clock and he sees that it's a quarter past twelve.

He hurries to the front door before the knocking wakes his ma. Pauses, wiping his hands on his apron. He doesn't want whoever's there to knock again; but he can't figure out who it might be. He undoes the chain and straightens the cross, his eyes falling briefly on the postcard of Jesus. If it's the Savior himself, the house is sadly a mess.

It's Jimmy Delancy.

"May I come inside, Albert?"

Delancy does not smile; his eyes black and dull, thick lines around them, a shadow casting him in grey.

"Ma's asleep."

Delancy opens the screen door and lets himself in.

Delancy's nodding the whole way from the front entrance to the big chair, where Delancy sits.

"I didn't come to see your mother."

He extends a hand to take Delancy's hat.

"I won't be staying."

Delancy takes a breath. "Albert," Delancy says, "you know I've been disappointed in you. We won't go into why, that's been covered enough."

He won't listen to a lecture. Not now, not anymore.

"Listen, Jimmy—"

"I've come to say thank you, Albert. You saved my Kara's wedding."

Ears go hot. Says nothing.

"And I won't forget it." Delancy reaches into his coat, pulls out a black leather wallet. "I want to give you something for your effort. In addition to the cost."

Delancy removing two one hundred dollar bills.

He thinks he might be sick, and the wash of weariness sprays up from his belly and into his head. At the river, just two nights before, he'd laid on the cold stones, his insides like the black current, unstoppable.

"No."

The thin face that has watched him over so many hands of cards, over so many Sunday sermons and dinners, that has seen him as baby and boy, falls loose for a moment, as if the muscles in Delancy's face have suddenly collapsed.

"What?" Delancy says. "All right. Three hundred then."

He feels suddenly OK again, a softness in his gut; and he's sad for Delancy, his wife dead, sitting in the chair of his late best friend.

"Just go, Jimmy," Albert says.

And the three bills between them, Delancy as if to speak and then he doesn't. Nodding, Delancy puts the bills back into his wallet, the wallet back into his coat, and Albert sees Delancy's hands are shaking. Delancy slowly stands and looks at him. The kitchen clock humming, water drops sliding through dishes. He wishes that Delancy would move toward the door.

Delancy breathes in fast. "You want a job, Albert?"

A dish settles and Albert glances over his shoulder to the sink. A dog barks. He cannot see out the window for the light in the kitchen.

Carefully. "I have a job, Jimmy. I don't want to wait tables."

"I need a chef."

Delancy's nodding again. Albert beginning to do the same.

"You'll have to train for a period."

Nodding; the room bobbing up and back behind Delancy, the Singer and the record player rising and falling, the pope into a blur.

"You slapped me."

"Yes." Eyes on Sandy and his da and the big boat with him as a boy. "For fuck's sake, Albert. I'm seventy-three years old and I've been up for forty-four hours. What's it going to be?"

"You'll give me free rein?"

"It occurred to me only today that I've eaten your food a hundred times and never had a bad bite. You want free rein? You, I trust."

And he knows Delancy means it and doesn't. Delancy means it as best as he can. He won't get free reign and he does not expect it. But to be an equal, to meet Delancy as a man.

He liked enough his job at Bobby's, but he likes cooking best. "Then sure, I'll do it, Jimmy. I'll take the job."

Delancy extends his hand. Albert takes it and for a moment he does not want to let it go.

"Say God bless to you mother."

Delancy fits the fedora on his head. "I'll let myself out."

And he does. Jimmy Delancy out the house, down darkened streets he'd walked before Albert was born.

He's between the kitchen and the front room, and behind him the tape player's building a reel. He turns from the cross and the postcard, turns from the LP cover and the basket and his da's old chair, and he steps back into the kitchen, a lemon wedge sliding beneath his foot.

The music building.

Your father has everything to do with this. Your mother

loves you more than Jesus Christ himself. It was maybe that love did not take the clearest path, or that the clearest path was not at the first apparent. When he was nine, they'd left for a night ride from Leeville, out into the Gulf, the whole family staying with Jim Teddy, who at the time was assistant harbor master. Jim Teddy in the wheel house, Sandy and Albert watching the wake, his parents facing the wavering lights of the shoreline. And he'd caught his parents kissing, really kissing, and Sandy snuck over and stuck his head up between them, and Albert had gone up to where the bow was splitting the waves, and the stars made a path through the sky.

The music coming through. He looks around quickly, to see that he is alone, and then he lifts his left eyebrow, and then he lifts his right. He lifts slightly his left leg. Lowers it. Lifts slightly his right. Right, and then again his left. And the eyebrows, and the arms folded out in front, and the belly now waving up in the glass of the window over the sink. A modest jig, in the kitchen of the uptown shotgun house, as a late-night train rattles down St. Charles toward the Quarter, and the stray coming up the street, licking at her fur.

ACKNOWLEDGMENTS

Thank you Andrea Barrett, David Haynes, Kate Lacey, Amey Miller, Michael Congdon, and Joseph Olshan. The best of this book is filled with them.

Thanks Jim Marcovitz, Pete Turchi and Ehud Havazelet, for all kinds of help.

This book would not exist without Ashley McKinney— in New Orleans, riding the streetcar, walking the Quarter, talking, writing, imagining Albert. I and this book owe a great debt of gratitude.

Thank you Cecile Engel and Lori Milken.

Thank you Bernard J. Plansky, for the stories and music. Thank you Dan Chuba, Katherine Holmes, Lisa Muscat, Memsy Price, and John Shapiro.

And thank you to the Squaw Valley Community of Writers, Warren Wilson College, the North Carolina School of the Arts, Writers' Conferences and Festivals, the Virginia Center for the Contemporary Arts, the Chenango Valley Workshops, the Arts and Letters Workshops, the Writers Room in New York City, and, in New Orleans, Mary Lou Eichorn and the Williams Research Center, and Rosemary James and Faulkner House Books.